DEC 2 1

CRIMINAL MISCHIEF

BOOKS BY STUART WOODS

FICTION

Criminal Mischief*

Foul Play*

Class Act*

Double Jeopardy*

Hush-Hush*

Shakeup*

Choppy Water*

Hit List*

Treason*

Stealth*

Contraband*

Wild Card*

A Delicate Touch*

Desperate Measures*

Turbulence*

Shoot First*

Unbound*

Quick & Dirty*

Indecent Exposure*

Fast & Loose*

Below the Belt*

Sex, Lies & Serious Money*

Dishonorable Intentions*

Family Jewels*

Scandalous Behavior*

Foreign Affairs*

Naked Greed*

Hot Pursuit*

Insatiable Appetites*

Paris Match*

Cut and Thrust*

Carnal Curiosity*

Standup Guy*

Doing Hard Time*

Unintended Consequences*

Collateral Damage*

Severe Clear*

Unnatural Acts*

D.C. Dead*

Son of Stone*

Bel-Air Dead*

Strategic Moves*

Santa Fe Edge†

Lucid Intervals*

Kisser*

Hothouse Orchid‡

Loitering with Intent*

Mounting Fears§

Hot Mahogany*

Santa Fe Dead†

Beverly Hills Dead

Shoot Him If He Runs*

Fresh Disasters*

Short Straw†

Dark Harbor*

Iron Orchid‡

Two Dollar Bill*

The Prince of Beverly Hills

Reckless Abandon*

Capital Crimes§

Dirty Work*

Blood Orchid‡

The Short Forever*

Orchid Blues‡

Cold Paradise*   Dead Eyes

L.A. Dead*   L.A. Times

The Run§   Santa Fe Rules†

Worst Fears Realized*   New York Dead*

Orchid Beach‡   Palindrome

Swimming to Catalina*   Grass Roots§

Dead in the Water*   White Cargo

Dirt*   Deep Lie§

Choke   Under the Lake

Imperfect Strangers   Run Before the Wind§

Heat   Chiefs§

COAUTHORED BOOKS

Bombshell** (with Parnell Hall)

Skin Game** (with Parnell Hall)

The Money Shot** (with Parnell Hall)

Barely Legal†† (with Parnell Hall)

Smooth Operator** (with Parnell Hall)

TRAVEL

A Romantic's Guide to the Country Inns of Britain and Ireland (1979)

MEMOIR

Blue Water, Green Skipper

*A Stone Barrington Novel
†An Ed Eagle Novel
‡A Holly Barker Novel
§A Will Lee Novel
**A Teddy Fay Novel
††A Herbie Fisher Novel

CRIMINAL MISCHIEF

STUART WOODS

G. P. PUTNAM'S SONS
NEW YORK

PUTNAM
—EST. 1838—

G. P. PUTNAM'S SONS
Publishers Since 1838
An imprint of Penguin Random House LLC
penguinrandomhouse.com

Hardcover ISBN: 9780593331729
Ebook ISBN: 9780593331736

Printed in the United States of America
1st Printing

Book design by Laura K. Corless
Title page: Desert landscape © kamin Jaroensuk / shutterstock.com

This is a work of fiction. Names, characters, places, and incidents either are the product of
the author's imagination or are used fictitiously, and any resemblance to actual persons,
living or dead, businesses, companies, events, or locales is entirely coincidental.

This book is for
Stephanie Walters,
with affection.

CRIMINAL MISCHIEF

1

Stone Barrington stood at the bar at P.J. Clarke's, already half a drink ahead of Dino Bacchetti. He and Dino had been NYPD detective partners many moons ago, when they were young and reckless, until it had been suggested by his superiors, with emphasis, that Stone's talents lay elsewhere (anywhere but the NYPD) and he had decamped to the law. He already had a law degree from NYU in his pocket, and an old classmate brought him aboard at the firm of Woodman & Weld, while he crammed for the bar exam. Dino had opted for the whole thirty years and now found himself the police commissioner of New York City. They dined together often.

Not this evening, though. Stone's iPhone buzzed in his pocket, and he reached for it. "It's Stone."

"It's Dino. It's not happening tonight. Big emergency, hands to hold. Tomorrow?"

"Sure, but at Patroon. I'm already at Clarke's."

"At seven." They both hung up.

"Dumped again?" a female voice said from somewhere below him. "He or she?"

He looked down to find a small, dark-haired young woman in a sharp black dress, complete with cleavage, newly perched on a stool he had marked for himself.

"He," Stone replied. "Emergency."

"That's what they all say," she said. "Does that make you available for a drink?"

"I've already got one," Stone replied.

"I haven't."

"What is your pleasure?"

She swiveled toward the bartender. "Knob Creek on the rocks," she said, and it appeared in a flash. She raised her glass to Stone. "Your liver," she said.

"I'll drink to that and yours, too, since you have such good taste in bourbon."

"Do you possess a name?" she asked. "And if so, what is it?"

"I do, and it is Stone Barrington. What about you?"

"I do, as well. Tink Dorsey, a gift from my older brother who liked to say that I was no bigger than a Tinker Toy. I'm five feet, two inches tall. Wasn't that your next question?"

"Well, no," Stone said.

"Then 36-C," she said. "That would have been your second question."

"I thought about it, then decided it was more polite not to ask."

"Ah, an explorer," she said, getting a laugh. "In what vineyard do you toil?"

"The law, though my partners often question how hard. Your turn again."

"I'm about six chapters away from being a novelist," she said. "Previously I have written only for money."

"And will again, I'm sure. After all, you're only six chapters away."

"And many miles," she said.

"You've just got a slight case of first-novel-itis."

"A critical case."

"You'll handle it."

"We'll see. Does your phone call mean you're free for dinner?"

"Yes. How about you?"

"If you're buying."

"I could not fail to feed a starving writer." He ushered her back to the dining room, where the headwaiter found them a table and menus.

They had finished their dinner and a dessert.

"Would you like a cognac?" Stone asked.

"Yes, thank you, but I'd like it at your place. I want to see how you live."

Stone did not drag his feet. "Certainly," he said, signing the bill.

Outside, he hailed a cab, since Fred, his factotum, was off for the night. Shortly, they were deposited at Stone's front door.

The beeping started as Stone was turning on lights.

"Want me to enter the code for you?" Tink asked.

"Sure." He gave her the code, and the beeping mercifully stopped. "Living room," he said. "Dining room beyond that."

"I hadn't expected a whole house," she said. "Nobody I know has a whole house."

"I inherited it from my great-aunt, my grandmother's sister," he said. "And then I spent every penny I had renovating it. Did most of the work myself."

"That must have taken years," she said.

"Centuries, or so it seemed. Come see the study. We'll find brandy there." He led her across the living room and into the smaller room, then he lit a fire, poured brandy, and pointed her at the sofa.

"What are these four paintings?" Tink asked, pointing.

"Those are by my mother, Matilda Stone. She became very well-known after her death."

Tink walked over and tried to tilt one. "Oh, I thought it wasn't quite straight."

"It's firmly fastened to the wall. They were stolen once, and when I got them back I took pains to see that it wouldn't happen again."

She pointed at a small bronze sculpture. "May I pick this up?"

"Sure."

"What is it?"

"It's a sculpture of a horse soldier by Frederic Remington, called *The Sergeant*."

"Very handsome." She replaced the bronze, then went and sat down and accepted a cognac. "What a nice room!"

"Thank you." He sat down beside her

"I trust you can see my cleavage from there?"

"Indeed, and a lovely sight it is."

"I'm told it's my best feature."

"I'll have to have a look at your other features before I can decide," he said.

She laughed that pleasant little laugh again. "A little more cognac, and I'm sure that can be arranged." She tilted her head back, so he could lean down from his height and kiss her. When he did, she placed a hand on the back of his neck and pulled him into the kiss. Neither of them let go for some time.

She finally came up for air. "Your tour is incomplete," she said. "You haven't shown me your bedroom, yet."

He took her hand and pulled her to her feet. "That, too, can be arranged."

Much later a slight rustle of bedclothes woke him. "Must you go?"

"Yes, I must, but we can do it again. Zip me."

He felt his way, then zipped.

"I left my card on the bedside table." She kissed him and pulled up the covers. "Now, you go back to sleep." She left the door open, and he could hear her footsteps down the stairs. He drifted off.

He was awakened by the bell of the dumbwaiter, bringing breakfast, but he had to run for the bathroom first. That work done, he got into a light robe and got back into bed, noticing that her card was not on the other bedside table. Never mind, he'd find her.

At mid-morning, he showered and shaved, then dressed and went downstairs to his office. On the way, he passed the study and noticed that the lights were still on. He walked in and checked his mother's paintings, a nervous habit he'd acquired after they had been stolen and recovered. They were still in place.

He turned toward the light switch, and as he did, he stopped. Something was missing. He checked the paintings again, then turned his attention to the bookcase. The Remington bronze was gone.

S tone slid in behind his desk, picked up the phone, and speed-
dialed Dino.

"Bacchetti."

"I want to report a robbery."

"Normally, I would transfer you to burglary, but my interest is piqued. Who robbed you?"

"A small, dark-haired woman with wonderful breasts—wonderful everything, actually."

"I hope you got something of value in return."

"You know the little Remington bronze in my study?"

"*The Sergeant*? I've coveted it for years."

"That."

"What is its value?"

"I paid twenty-five grand for it, at auction, some years ago."

"I suppose you didn't get that much for it, in exchange for services rendered."

"You could say that. I mean, it was spectacular, but not *that* spectacular."

"Does this robber have a name?"

"Let's put it this way, she used one: Tink Dorsey."

"I don't suppose you have a photograph."

"We didn't get that far."

"So, shall I put out an APB for a short, dark-haired woman with great tits, carrying a small but expensive sculpture?"

"You think that would get some action?"

"I think a lot of street cops would be on the lookout for the tits."

"Yeah, you might need to rephrase."

"I think we'd better just post it on our stolen art page. The art boys probably even have a photograph of it on file."

"Go."

"We still on for dinner at Patroon?"

"Sure."

"I don't suppose you'll be bringing Tink Dorsey."

"Not unless you capture her." They both hung up.

His secretary, Joan Robertson, buzzed him.

"Yes?"

"Someone who says her name is 'Tink' is on two."

Stone hesitated, then decided not to bring up *The Sergeant*. He pressed the button. "Good morning!"

"I trust you slept well for the rest of the night."

"I did. I would have called to thank you, but I couldn't find your card."

"Oh, shit. I forgot. I used them all up, gotta get some reprinted. Here's my number." She gave him one with a 917 area code, a cell phone.

"Got it."

"Am I interrupting anything?"

"Only the practice of law. You want to join a friend and me for dinner?"

"The friend who dumped you last night?"

"One and the same."

"Love to."

"Can we meet at Patroon?" He gave her the address. "Seven?"

"See you there. How are we dressing?"

"I'm wearing a necktie."

"Then I won't."

"It would just get in the way of what some have called your best feature," he said.

She laughed and hung up. He did like that laugh.

Stone got there first, then Dino walked in right behind Tink, who was already laughing. They put her in the booth between them.

"Did you two get introduced?"

"We did not," she said.

"Tink Dorsey, this is Dino Bacchetti."

She shook his hand. "Oh, I know that name. Aren't you the DA, or something?"

"I'm the police commissioner for the City of New York," Dino replied, flashing his badge, "and you're under arrest."

She laughed. "And what for? I haven't had time to steal the silver yet."

"For the theft of a valuable work of art," Dino said. "A small Remington sculpture called *The Sergeant*."

She reached into her bag. For a moment, Stone thought she might come up with a gun, but instead she came up with the Remington and set it on the table. "You mean this?"

"That's what I mean," Dino said. "I take it you're confessing."

"Well, I was listing to the right when I left Stone's house last night, and I needed some ballast."

It was Dino's turn to laugh.

"Really, Stone, I only borrowed it for the night, just so I could look at it some more. You didn't need to call the cops, let alone the police commissioner."

"I always go directly to the top," Stone said.

"I like that in a man."

Dino barged in. "Are you dropping the charges, Stone?"

Stone hefted *The Sergeant* in his hands and inspected it thoroughly. It had the right number stamped into the bronze. "I guess I have no alternative," he said.

"Gee, thanks," Tink said. "What a compliment!"

"You were a bad girl, and you gave me a fright," Stone explained.

"I guess I was, but my heart's in the right place."

"I can't deny that," Stone said.

They ordered.

Fred was waiting outside with the Bentley, and it was raining. They piled in.

"This is gorgeous," Tink said, stroking the leather. "If I'd known you drove a Bentley, I would have stolen the car, instead."

"Home, Fred," Stone said. "Tink, that's Fred in the front seat. Fred, she's Tink Dorsey."

"Good evening, Ms. Dorsey."

"So far," she replied.

"Can you manage to stay the whole night?" Stone asked.

"What's the matter, you afraid I'll steal something else?"

"Only my heart."

"I was aiming farther south, but I'll take what I can get."

Fred pulled into the garage.

"An indoor Bentley!" Tink said. "This gets better and better!"

Upstairs, they went to their respective dressing rooms and emerged simultaneously, equally naked. Stone yanked the covers back, and they fell into bed.

"Just think of this as a continuation of last night," Tink said. "Pretend I never left."

Stone's position muffled his reply.

"Don't talk, sweetie," she said. "You're doing just fine," she breathed.

It took half an hour to wear themselves out, then they slept. Tink woke up first; her head was in his lap, so she didn't have far to go.

Stone made a noise.

She stopped. "Sorry about that."

"I think it was Helen Lawrenson who said, by way of instruction, 'It's like eating a banana, without leaving any teeth marks.'"

"I'll remember that," she said, then returned to her work.

Stone came explosively.

She crawled up and put her head on his shoulder. "I'll bet you think you're done for the night," she said.

"Absolutely."

"Don't count on it."

3

The dumbwaiter bell went off. Tink sat bolt upright and wide-eyed. "Is the house on fire?"

"No, that's breakfast."

"Breakfast makes a noise?"

"Every morning about this time," Stone said. "It's best to just get used to it. Changing it would mess up everything." He pushed the cart over to the bed and put a tray on her belly.

"What am I having?"

"English scrambled eggs, breakfast sausages, half a Wolferman's English muffin, orange juice, and coffee. If you want something else, you have to place your order at bedtime."

"I was busy at the time," she said.

He reached across her, took a remote control from the bedside chest and pressed a button. She rose to meet her tray. "Fantastic," she said. "What are English scrambled eggs?"

"Cooked very slowly with lots of butter until they're creamy, but not runny. Americans overcook eggs, and they lose most of their flavor."

She took her fork and tried them. "Mmmmm," she said. "What a surprise." She tried a sausage. "You know what I'm having next time?"

"Wait, I'll get a pencil."

"Don't bother, I'm having exactly this."

Stone switched on the TV, to *Morning Joe.*

"What is this?" she asked.

He explained to her about MSNBC.

"Don't you get Fox News?"

"I can, but I don't like being lied to."

"I thought it was MSNBC that did all the lying."

"That's because you were being lied to."

"Okay, it's your TV. I'll go along."

They gobbled down their breakfast.

"Who are all these people on TV?" she asked.

"People who don't appear on Fox News."

"Wait a minute, I get it. You're a Democrat?"

"Wrong. I'm a yellow-dog Democrat."

"What's that?"

"A Democrat who'd vote for a yellow dog before he'd vote for a Republican."

"Oh, well, I hardly ever vote, anyway," she said.

"Thank God for that."

"Something I don't get."

"Ask."

"You're rich, but you're a Democrat?"

"Well, there's me and George Soros and Warren Buffett and a few others."

"How'd you get all the money?"

"I got it the old-fashioned way. I inherited it."

"Your parents were rich?"

"No. I had a wife who had been married to a very rich man before me, and when she died, I inherited a chunk of her estate."

"What did she die of?"

"A shotgun."

Her face fell.

"Not mine. It belonged to a former lover of hers."

"So, you got rich honestly?"

"I'm afraid so. Do you find that surprising?"

"Sort of. I always thought rich people were sort of crooked."

"A lot of rich people are, I guess."

"What proportion?"

"About fifty-fifty, in my experience."

"How do you tell the difference?"

"The dishonest ones try to get you to be dishonest. They always have a hot stock tip or a horse race or a law that's fixed, or so they tell you. Sometimes they're running a Ponzi scheme."

"What's that?"

"It's named after a man named Ponzi. What he did was to talk people into investing with him, then sending them a fat check every month, but he wasn't investing their money. He was using the money of new investors to pay the old ones, and he kept a lot of it for himself."

"How can you tell if you're investing in a Ponzi scheme?"

"If you're getting a fat check every month, you're a victim. No investment company can return ten or fifteen percent."

"Suppose I invested in a company like that. Should I pull out?"

"As fast as you can."

"What if they won't return my money?"

"Oh, they will, but it will be the money of other investors. If they fail the payout, then you'll tell all your friends and they'll tell their friends, and pretty soon the Ponzi guy is either in jail or on a plane to Rio. He wants to keep the ball rolling."

"Ah, I see."

"Tink, have you invested in something that sounds like that?"

"Maybe."

"Tell me about it."

"You just told me. It sounds just like that."

"Do you get a monthly statement from these people?"

"Yes." She got out of bed, found her handbag, rummaged in it and brought Stone an envelope.

Stone looked at the return address: *One Vanderbilt Avenue.*

"Uh-oh," he said, and took a sheet of paper from the envelope.

"What 'uh-oh'?"

"Just a minute." Stone ran a finger down a column of figures. "You've got over three hundred thousand dollars invested with these people?"

"Not people, just the guy."

Stone looked at the letterhead. *Zanian Growth Fund, One Vanderbilt Avenue.*

"His name is Viktor Zanian. He's from an old New York Dutch family."

"Did you ever look him up in the phone book?"

"What phone book? There's no phone book anymore."

"Did you look on the Internet?"

"Yeah, he's got a sort of hidden website."

"I'll bet he does."

"Do you think he might be crooked?"

"Oh, yes, I think he might just be very crooked."

"Why?"

"For all the reasons I just told you, and one more."

"What's that?"

"Do you know what One Vanderbilt Avenue is?"

"An office building?"

"One Vanderbilt Avenue is the street address of Grand Central Station. This is a mail drop."

"A what?"

"It's a mailbox—a private service. You can rent one and use that address. Just don't ever try to visit his office."

"Oh, my God," she muttered.

Once at his desk, Stone called Charley Fox, with whom he was a partner in an investment firm, Triangle Investments, along with Mike Freeman, CEO of Strategic Services, the world's second-largest security firm.

"Morning, Charley, it's Stone."

"Morning, Stone."

"Charley, have you ever heard of a guy named Zanian?" He spelled it.

"I knew a guy named Viktor Zanian, who was at Goldman Sachs when I was."

"How would you characterize him?"

"Tricky," Charley replied. "I'd call him worse, if I had the evidence."

"What do you mean?"

"He left Goldman under a cloud, as they say, but I never understood what kind of cloud. There were rumors, all of them unfavorable, but I never got the whole story. Why are you asking?"

"A young lady of my acquaintance has an investment account with him, and she gets a fat check every month, more than her investment, three hundred grand, would support."

"Uh-oh. Sounds as though old Vik is running a Ponzi scheme."

"That's pretty much what I said when I heard. How do I get her out, clean?"

"Tell her to write him a letter on her printed letterhead, instructing him to close her accounts and wire the funds to her bank account. I'm assuming she has one. Tell her to make it friendly and nonconfrontational, just to say that she needs her funds immediately, but that she may be able to reinvest them with him later. She should send the letter by registered mail."

"And if there's no response, or an unsatisfactory one?"

"Tell her to call and write the Securities and Exchange Commission's enforcement department, but not to hold her breath. Also, if she gets her money back, tell her not to spread any rumors about Zanian. If she does, he'll trace them back to her."

"Is he the type to exact revenge?"

"He's the type who knows people who'll do it for him."

"Thanks, Charley."

"Anytime."

Stone hung up, dictated a letter for Tink's signature and told Joan to craft a letterhead for her and print it out for use. Then he called Tink.

"Hey, there," she said. "Missing any valuables?"

"I haven't checked, yet. But I'd like you to come by my office and sign a letter that I have written for you, getting you out of Zanian's fund."

"Oh, I won't be needing that."

"Why not?"

"I talked to Mr. Zanian this morning. He assured me that everything is running normally, and I had no need to be concerned about my investment with him."

"I'm sorry you did that, Tink. I did some checking on Mr. Zanian this morning, and it's important that you get out immediately."

"What did you hear?"

"Let's call it a case of worst fears realized."

"Oh, Stone, you're such an alarmist. I'm a very good judge of character, and Mr. Zanian is the genuine article."

"The genuine what?"

"Article. Good as gold."

"Do you have anyone's word for this, except that of Mr. Zanian?"

"I don't need that. I told you, I'm a great judge of character."

"That's what people always say when they are poor judges of character."

"Well, that's insulting."

"Please regard it as merely intuitive. Tink, if you're at home in bed, and the fire alarm goes off in your building, what would be your first move? Two choices: leave the building immediately or unplug the alarm?"

"You're just annoyed because I won't take your advice."

"I have a secondary recommendation."

"Oh, good. What is it?"

"When Mr. Zanian vanishes and your money with him, report it immediately to the Security and Exchange Commission's enforcement department. Oh, and don't call me."

"Goodbye, Stone," she said cheerfully, then hung up.

"SHIT!" Stone yelled into the ether.

"I beg your pardon?" Joan was standing in the doorway.

"Someone has just refused to take my advice."

"Who?"

"The person for whom you've typed up the letter."

"What shall I do with it?"

"Mail it to her, along with a stamped envelope addressed to Mr. Viktor—with a *k*—Zanian, One Vanderbilt Avenue."

"You know that's not a real address, don't you? It's a mail drop."

"It's where Mr. Zanian gets his mail, as far as I know."

"You know, I have an old college friend who's investing with that guy."

"Type her up a copy of the same letter and send it to her. The sooner she's out, the better."

"Do you have any evidence for this?"

"Charley Fox suspects him."

"Oh. In that case, I'll send her the letter." She left the room.

"SHIT!" Stone shouted again.

5

Stone called Dino.

"Bacchetti."

"You get anything on Viktor Zanian, yet?"

"I'll tell you about it over dinner."

"Do we have a dinner date?"

"We do now. Caravaggio, at seven."

"Who's buying?"

"You are."

"Didn't I buy last time?"

"Picky, picky, picky. See you at seven." Dino hung up.

Stone's drink and Dino arrived at the same moment, and it took only another moment to find Dino's Scotch. They drank.

"So," Dino said, "whaddaya hear from Tink Dorsey?"

"This isn't about Tink," Stone said.

"It is now. She's why you want to know about Zanian."

"Am I supposed to tell you something about Tink, or are you supposed to tell me something about Zanian?"

"You first."

"I checked with Charley Fox about Zanian and he gave the guy a bad report," Stone said. "So, I wrote a letter for Tink's signature, pulling her out of his fund, but she wouldn't sign it. Said she spoke with Zanian this morning, and he said everything was fine. And she believed him, because she's a 'great judge of character.'"

Dino laughed aloud. "Tink really said that?"

"She really did."

"And I bet you're not getting laid anymore."

"That hasn't come up yet."

"Don't worry, it will."

"You have a dark outlook, Dino," Stone said.

"That's because I'm a great judge of character."

Stone winced. "Whose character are we discussing at the moment?"

"Yours."

"Why mine?"

"You're the one who's trying to manipulate Tink."

"No, that would be Zanian."

"But he's a good guy. Tink said so."

"Whose judgment would you trust between Tink and Charley Fox, who worked at Goldman when Zanian got fired?"

"Does that make Charley a superior judge of character to Tink?"

"Charley was working on information gained in the same workplace. Tink is relying on charm."

"Isn't that how you got her into the sack?" Dino asked.

"That's different. We're talking money here."

"You think money had nothing to do with your getting Tink in the sack?"

"We didn't discuss money. At that time."

"Stone, any woman who took a stroll around your house would think you were awash in money."

"Now we're on the subject of my tastes in interior design?"

"Why not?"

"We were talking about Zanian."

"I thought we were talking about Tink," Dino said.

"We were talking about getting Tink and her money out of the clutches of Zanian, who is running a Ponzi scheme. At least, I was talking about that. And am. Do you want to see Tink lose all her hard-earned three hundred grand?"

"That brings up another matter. How did Tink earn the three hundred grand?"

"Dino, I don't care how she earned it. I just don't want her to lose it."

"As far as I can tell, the woman has no visible means of support."

"All the more important for her not to lose what she's got. And what do you care about the visibility of her support?"

"Do you think she's a high-priced hooker?" Dino asked.

"Do you know how long it would take a high-priced hooker to turn three hundred grand's worth of tricks?"

"No, do you?"

"No, and I don't care."

"But you care so deeply about Tink. Or, at least, about her three hundred grand."

"I don't care about her money."

"Then why are you so interested in protecting it?"

"I'm interested in protecting Tink. It's the same thing."

"I could argue that point," Dino said, "but not without another drink."

Stone raised a finger, and a waiter leapt into action.

Dino took a swig. "Where were we?"

"I've no idea," Stone said.

"Have you ever heard of somebody named Sean Delaney?" Dino asked.

"I may be a little confused by now," Stone said, "but I'm absolutely certain we were not talking about somebody named Sean Delaney."

"Why are you so certain we're not talking about Sean Delaney?"

"Because I've never heard of him."

"That doesn't mean we couldn't be talking about him."

"Is he related to Tink Dorsey?"

"You could say that."

"No, *you* could say that. I've never heard of him, so I can't say that."

"He's Tink's old man."

"In what context?"

"What do you mean, 'in what context'?"

25

"Is he her sugar daddy or her rich uncle?"

"Neither. He's a very slick con man."

"Why do I care?"

"Because you care about Tink."

"Is he trying to con her?"

"Of course not, why would he do that? He's her father."

Stone blinked. "Tink's father is a con man?"

"How do you think she got so good at it?"

"Are you saying that Tink is a con girl?"

"Con woman would be more au courant," Dino said, "not to mention woke."

"Why do you think this?"

"She could be in cahoots with Viktor Zanian."

"'In cahoots'? She's his victim or is about to be."

"Maybe."

"'Maybe'? Do you know something I don't know?"

"Stone, I know one hell of a lot that you don't know."

"Don't change the subject. We were on Viktor Zanian for a minute there."

"You didn't catch the six-thirty news tonight, did you?"

"No, I was coming here at that time. What did I miss?"

"You missed a very nice shot of the front door of Viktor Zanian's offices, if he has one, with a big chain and padlock on it, not to mention a warrant taped to the glass."

Stone started to say something, but Dino held up a hand. "The feds fell on Zanian from a great height," he said.

"When?"

"About the time you were tying your necktie."

"Has Tink heard?"

"I've no idea."

Stone's phone buzzed in his pocket, and he fished it out and peered at the screen. "It's Tink," he said.

"Uh-oh."

S tone pressed the button. "Hello?"

"'Hello'? Is that all you've got to say?"

"So far," Stone replied. "What's up?"

"You can say that to me?"

"I just made the attempt. Listen, we're just sitting down to dinner. Can we talk later?"

"'Later'? You think that will do?"

"Tink, this is your phone call. What is it about?"

"Did you watch the evening news?"

"No, I was dressing to go out about that time."

"What kind of lawyer are you, anyway?"

"One who dresses before going out to dinner."

"Where are you?"

"I'd tell you, if you promised not to come here, but you'd come anyway, wouldn't you?"

"In my current state of mind, yes, probably."

"What is your current state of mind?"

Tink searched for a word. "Bereft," she said, finally.

"Have you been left in a basket on somebody's doorstep?"

"This is no time to make bad jokes."

"I'm doing the best I can with the straight lines I'm being given. Toss me another one, and I'll try to improve."

"You knew this was going to happen, didn't you?"

"What has happened? Sorry, I'm working without a net here."

"Zanian has happened."

"I messengered you an envelope at midafternoon. Have you opened it and read the contents?"

"Not yet."

"This would be a good time. Call me back when you've read and digested it." He hung up.

"How bad is it?" Dino asked.

"Bad. I can't get her to speak the words."

"Hard to imagine her at a loss for words."

"Not exactly a loss. She just can't bring herself to speak them in the proper order." His phone rang. "Hello?"

"This is so typical," she hissed.

"You haven't known me long enough to know what is typical for me."

"Trying to weasel out of it. Typical lawyer."

"Did you read the document?"

Silence.

"The one with my signature at the bottom?"

More silence.

"I believe I expressed my concern that you were dealing with a dishonest person and should extricate your funds from his grasp at the earliest possible moment."

"I don't see the word 'dishonest' in this document."

"I believe I gave you the best advice I could in the circumstances, but you assured me that Mr. Zanian is 'good as gold.' I believe that was the expression you used."

"I knew you would throw that back at me."

"Then you're a better judge of character than I realized."

"That, too."

"How can I help you, Tink? Right now, I mean."

"I need a course of action."

"I believe my recommended course of action was included in my letter."

"That's useless to me now."

"Perhaps it would have been more useful to you at two o'clock this afternoon, when you signed for the letter then didn't bother to open and read it."

"It's useless."

"Good legal advice is always useless, until it is employed. If you ignore it, as you did, bad things can happen." Stone held his hand over the phone and said to Dino. "I think tears will happen about now."

Tink began to bawl. "You bastard!" she screamed.

"Tink, please get some rest and call me tomorrow, and we'll see what can be done. Good night." He hung up and switched off the phone.

"What can you possibly do tomorrow?" Dino asked.

"Absolutely nothing, but maybe she'll be in a better frame of mind to deal with it."

"I wouldn't count on it," Dino said, handing him the menu.

"I'll have the risotto del mare," Stone said. "And I will choose the wine, because I'm paying for it."

"I'll be happy with the Montrachet," Dino said.

"My purpose in life is not to make you happy," Stone said, "at least, not *that* happy. You can get just as drunk on a nice California chardonnay."

"You'd like that, wouldn't you? To get me drunk?"

"Not particularly, but you drunk is better than Tink sober."

S he waited until he was in the middle of breakfast to call.

Stone picked up the phone. "Not until after breakfast," he said, then hung up and finished breakfast.

She rang again.

"I'm not even dressed yet," he said.

"I don't care. I need to know what to do."

"I included instructions about that in my letter. They still apply."

"What is the SEC going to do for me?"

"Put you on a list—a longer list than it would have been yesterday—and if they ever convict Zanian and get some of the money back, you'll get some of it."

"How long will that take?"

"A year or two, depending on how long it takes to catch Zanian and how much money he has left."

"Isn't that hopeless?"

"Maybe not. Would you rather have a third of your money back or none at all?"

"What kind of choice is that?"

"One where you have some money and another where you have none."

"You're laughing at me, aren't you?"

"I won't entertain that question. Anything else?"

"No."

"Then you'd better start communicating with the SEC."

"Will you do that for me?"

"You can't afford my services. Do it yourself."

She hung up more quietly this time. Stone got into a shower.

B ack at his desk, Joan buzzed him. "Dino on one."

Stone pressed the button. "Yo."

"What does that mean?"

"Nobody knows. It doesn't mean yes; it doesn't mean no."

"I suppose you've heard from Miss Tink this morning."

"Yes."

"Is she any better?"

"I think she has finally grasped the reality of her situation, and that's probably something new for her."

"I guess that means she really was conned. Did you see the CNN shots this morning of Zanian getting off a Gulfstream in Rio?"

"I missed that. Did he steal enough to buy a Gulfstream?"

"The little one, which isn't so little."

"Anything on how much he walked away with?"

"There was less than half a million in his New York bank account, which means he moved it offshore early on."

"Yeah," Stone said. "Gulfstream won't give you an airplane if you give them a bad check."

"I guess he could have bought a used one, like you."

"I guess, but it wouldn't be as nice as mine. Has anybody tried to kidnap Zanian yet?" Stone asked.

"Nothing out there about that. You think he's a candidate for kidnapping?"

"I'd bet there's a team being assembled now, not that it would do them any good. The money is probably in Macao or the Dutch East Indies by now."

"Well, they could have the fun of torturing him for the account numbers," Dino said.

"Tink would gleefully join in that activity."

"Well, after all, he told her he was a good guy, didn't he? The memory of all that will light her fuse. Are you going to help her?"

"What can I do, apart from joining the kidnap team?"

"Isn't there some lawyer thing you can work?"

"It's hard to sue a guy who's in a country with no extradition treaty with the U.S. About all you could do is shoot him, and you can't extradite a corpse or its money, either."

"This just in," Dino said. "Reuters is reporting that Zanian could have got away with as much as six hundred million dollars."

"Then he could afford a *new* Gulfstream."

"He probably borrowed the money," Dino said.

"If that's the case, his bank already has people out there looking to steal the airplane back, although they'd call it a repo. No, if Zanian is smart enough to steal that much money, then he's smart enough to hide it, and in an airplane is a good place."

"What would he do for ready cash?"

"A ready bank down the street from wherever he is. Also, he would have bolted a concealed safe to the airframe, so he can bribe his way into his next destination. I had a client once who was a director of a big pharma company, and they sent him on a tour of their African branches with three hundred grand in a safe, just for bribes. There wasn't much left when he got back."

"Well," Dino said. "It's nice to hear that the American dollar is still good for *something*."

"Of course, he's probably bought a lot of Bitcoin," Stone said.

"What do you know about Bitcoin?"

"Not a thing. I don't understand it. I just threw that in because it sounds good."

"Just as I thought."

"I just thought of something," Dino said.

"Dare I ask?"

"How are you going to get laid, if you can't get Tink's money back?"

"I was afraid you'd bring that up."

"What are the chances?"

"Pretty near zero right now."

"Well, you can always consult the little black book and dredge up somebody from the past."

"The past is past; I'd rather keep looking ahead."

"That's a good excuse for not scoring. Viv has a friend she keeps talking about hooking you up with," Dino said. "She gets home tomorrow. Want me to ask her about it?"

"Not yet. Let's wait until I'm really desperate."

"You sound really desperate now."

"All right, mention it to her. Does this woman have a name?"

"Kitty Crosse, with an *e*."

"Sounds like a sex position."

"That's up to you two. I'll see what Viv can do."

"See ya." Stone hung up.

Immediately, Joan buzzed him. "Tink for you on one."

"Tell her I had a heart attack and died."

"She said that she promises this will be her last call to you."

"That might be worth taking," Stone said. He pushed the button. "You promise this is the last call?"

"It is. I just want to apologize for hanging all this on you. You tried to help me, and I blew you off. I want you to know I'm sorry. You gave me good advice, and I ignored it."

Stone was taken aback. "You're serious?"

"I am. Can we have dinner soon?"

"What for?"

"Well, if you won't see me, who am I going to fuck?"

"Tink, as much fun as that sounds, I'm going to have to pass. I'm seeing someone else now."

"Oh, really? Who?"

"I'd rather not bring her into this conversation. I appreciate your apology, and I wish you well with getting your money back. Goodbye."

"*Whaaa—?*"

Stone hung up before she could finish the word.

8

Stone sat in the booth at Patroon and waited for the Bacchettis and Viv's friend Kitty to arrive. God knew it was not his first blind date, but it had been a while, and he was a little nervous.

Then Viv walked through the door, and behind her, mostly concealed by Viv, was someone taller, with darker hair and a bare shoulder. That was all he could see.

He slid across his seat and stood up out of courtesy and for a better view. He took in a quick breath. Viv had moved in such a way as to reveal a tall, dark-haired woman in a low-cut, strapless dress and, probably, very high heels, since she was half a head taller than Viv, who wasn't short.

"Stone," Viv said, smiling gleefully, "I want you to meet Kitty Crosse."

"With an *e*," Kitty said, reaching out for Stone's hand, giving him a glimpse of red nail polish that matched her lipstick.

Dino stood behind her, laughing at Stone's reaction.

"It's a pleasure to meet you, Kitty," Stone managed to say. Her long fingers encircled his hand.

"Please have a seat." Everybody did, then ordered drinks.

"A Moscow Mule," Kitty said.

"I've forgotten what that is," Stone said as the waiter wrote it down.

"Vodka, ginger beer, and lime juice," Kitty said. "Maybe a couple of other things. I can't remember."

"The bartender will know," Stone said.

"Viv tells me you're an attorney," Kitty said.

"For my sins. What about you?"

"I'm divorced."

"For a living?"

"Divorce pays very well, if you do it right," she replied.

"Who was your attorney?"

"Herbert Fisher—a partner of yours, I hear."

"You were certainly in good hands," Stone said, trying not to look down her cleavage.

"It's all right," she said.

"You read minds, do you?"

"I follow gazes. If I didn't want you to admire my breasts, I wouldn't have worn this dress."

"That's frank and forthright," Stone said.

"Two of my better qualities, though some men are put off by them. The qualities, not my breasts."

Viv spoke up, "Perhaps you two can arrange a private viewing, later."

"That's certainly a possibility," Kitty said, while Stone quietly choked on his bourbon.

"I look forward to it," he finally managed to say. He was saved by the arrival of the menus.

After dinner they made their way out of the restaurant.

"I have my car," Stone said. "May I drive you home?"

"It's early," she said. "I understand you have a handsome house. May I see it?"

"You may," Stone said, helping her into the Bentley.

"This is a beautiful car," Kitty said, stroking the leather seat. "I've been thinking of buying something I can be chauffeured in. Do you recommend it?"

"I do, unreservedly. You can even order it armored—if your divorce was an unpleasant one. Home, Fred."

"I have a dog named Fred," Kitty said, quietly.

"Mine is named Bob," Stone said.

"And where is he tonight?"

"Where he is every night, asleep by the fire."

They pulled into the garage. "Now, I don't have one of these," Kitty said, looking around.

"Buy the house next door, or I'm sure there's a good garage in your neighborhood that would be proud to have a Bentley as a tenant. They like parking them up front, where the other tenants can see them. An attempt to justify their prices, I expect."

They got off the elevator and walked into the living room.

"How very nice," Kitty said. "Viv didn't overstate your virtues."

"I don't claim to be virtuous," Stone said, showing her into the study.

"Living well is the best virtue," Kitty said. "You seem to have mastered that."

"I do the best I can," Stone said, handing her the requested martini.

She followed his gaze. "I see I'm holding your attention," she said.

"You certainly are."

"I promised you a viewing, I believe."

"You did, but I won't hold you to it."

She stood up, reached behind her, and pulled down the zipper. Her dress made a puddle at her feet. She was wearing only a thong now, and her shoes.

"I'm impressed," Stone said.

Kitty sat down and crossed her legs. "I'd be worried about you if you weren't. Do you sleep on this sofa?"

"There's a master suite upstairs," he said.

"Let's have a look at that." She picked up her dress, slung it over a shoulder, and followed him upstairs, then looked around. "Just the sort of thing I expected." She handed him her dress. "Hang this somewhere, please."

Stone relieved her of the garment and hung it in the dressing room. By the time he returned, the thong and her shoes had been dealt with, too.

"I promised Viv I'd tell her what you're like in bed," she said, working on his buttons.

Stone gave her every assistance.

Half an hour later, Kitty said, "I'll give Viv a good report on you."

"I'm flattered," Stone replied.

She threw a leg over and mounted him. "Are you good for another round?" she asked.

"Let's find out," Stone said, as she slipped him inside her.

Stone next knew consciousness when the dumbwaiter bell went off.

"Are we under arrest?" Kitty asked sleepily.

"Not yet. That means that breakfast is on the way up."

"When did you order breakfast?"

"Last night. I sent a note to the cook in the dumbwaiter."

"How clever of you. About a lot of things," she said.

"I just followed your lead," he replied, "and I enjoyed where it went."

"So did I," she replied.

Stone set the breakfast aside and reengaged.

9

Stone lay back with Kitty's head resting on his chest. "It's Saturday," he said. "You don't have to go to work, do you?"

"Being a divorcée doesn't make a lot of demands on my time. Would you go shopping with me today?"

"I'd be delighted. What will you be shopping for?"

"A Bentley," she said.

"I expect you'll want to go home and change."

"Not really," she said, picking up her handbag, reaching inside and coming out with a silk dress. "I'll borrow a shower, though."

"Right through there," Stone said, pointing. "Let me know if you need anything." He got up and headed for his own shower. He shaved, dried his hair, and put on khaki trousers, loafers, and a checked shirt, then got into a blue blazer. He emerged as Kitty did. She looked fresh and new, and he liked the dress.

Fred had the car out front, and Stone installed Kitty in the rear seat next to him. As he got into the car he saw a black Mercedes parked half a block down the street with the motor running. It didn't mean anything, he thought, but it was noticeable, for reasons he couldn't entirely fathom.

They were driven over to Eleventh Avenue, where the car dealerships had collected, and to the Bentley showroom. "I like that one," Kitty said as they entered. The car was parked in the center of the showroom.

"It's a Flying Spur, like mine."

Kitty walked slowly around the car and paused at the window sticker.

A salesman materialized at her elbow. "May I help you, ma'am?"

"You may sell me this car, if we can agree on a price."

"Will you require bank financing, ma'am?"

"I'll write you a check."

"One moment, please." The man went to a phone and spoke briefly. He jotted something on a piece of paper, hung up, and handed it to her. "That includes a generous discount, and all taxes and other charges."

"Done," she said. She walked over to his desk, sat down, produced an alligator-bound checkbook from her purse, wrote a check, and signed it. "There you are," she said. "I'll have to move some money on Monday morning, but you can cash it by noon, I expect."

Stone knew the salesman and saw him hesitate. "I'll vouch for Ms. Crosse," he said.

"I can have it cleaned and ready to go in an hour," he said to Kitty.

She handed him a card. "Just drop it off at my building and

leave the keys with the doorman," she said. "Nice doing business with you."

"A pleasure, ma'am. Mr. Barrington, thank you for the referral."

Stone walked her back to his car, where Fred stood, braced, with the door open. "That was quickly done," he said to Kitty.

"If you want something," she said, "why fuck around?"

Stone hoped her check would clear. As they pulled into traffic, Stone looked at the front rearview mirror and saw a black Mercedes pull in behind them, a few car lengths back.

"Does your ex-husband drive a black Mercedes?" he asked.

She looked at him askance. "How would you know that?"

"Because there's a black Mercedes following us a ways back. It was waiting outside my house when we left."

"How many people in it?" she asked without looking back.

"Two," Stone replied.

"He's been abroad," she said. "I guess he's back."

"How concerned should I be about that?"

"What do you mean?"

"When people follow other people around, they usually have some sort of intent. Does he go around armed?"

"He has a license to do so, but I've no way of knowing if he is at the moment."

"Did he have the habit of carrying?"

"Now and then. He would never tell me why."

"What's his name?"

"Harry Hillman," she replied. "He's British."

"Is he an American citizen?"

"No, he's far too snobbish about being an Englishman."

"Would you like to have him thrown out of the country?"

"He's been pretty decent about the divorce, so I don't think so. If he gets to be a nuisance, I may ask your help in that regard. Can you really do that?"

"I might be able to assist him on his way. I just don't want him to shoot me between now and then. Has he ever shot anyone?"

"He used to brag about having shot a man when he was in the army, but I never knew whether to believe him."

"Whose army?"

"The queen's."

"Did he brag about other things you doubted?"

"He certainly had a tendency to brag, but never to the extent that I doubted him. It was always something schoolboyish like a fistfight. He would brag that he had knocked a man out with a single punch, that sort of thing."

"I must remember not to let him land a punch," Stone said. "What size is he?"

She looked at him. "Size? Really?"

"Oh, please. Height and weight will do."

"Sorry. Six feet four, two-twenty, or thereabouts."

"I'm sorry to hear it," Stone muttered. "Where will you park the car?" he asked, seeking to change the subject.

"There's a garage in the building, and I own two spots. The doorman will know." She got out her cell phone. "I'll give him a heads-up." She did so.

"How did you come to marry an Englishman?" Stone asked.

"Well, I was in England," she replied, "and it just sort of happened. He can be quite charming if he feels like it."

Stone kept checking the rearview mirror. They might have been towing the black Mercedes, he thought. "Where to now?"

"You can let me off at Bloomingdale's. I can find my way home from there."

"You don't want company?" He glanced over his shoulder.

"Still there?"

"Still there," he replied.

"I'll manage," she said.

"Ask your doorman to recommend a driver for your new car."

"Good idea."

He dropped her at Bloomingdale's and, as he drove away, got a pretty good look at the large man in the passenger seat. It would be harder for the man to sneak up on him now.

S tone called a familiar number.

"Herb Fisher."

"Hi, it's Stone."

"Hi, there. It's been a while. What's up?"

"Kitty Crosse is up."

"She's something, ain't she? Too bad the bar association frowns on sex with clients."

"Fortunately, she's not my client."

"I envy you your availability."

"What kind of divorce did she have?"

"She got it done. I think her husband was a little afraid of her. His attorney certainly was. Meetings were short."

"What do you think of the husband?"

"I think he's the kind of guy who likes to beat up smaller guys, which in his case, includes just about everybody."

"He's a bully, then?"

"That's what we used to call them in the neighborhood."

"Is he also a coward?"

"A coward?"

"They say that bullies are really cowards."

"Probably some truth in that."

"Any advice on dealing with the husband?"

"Yeah, get in the first punch, and give it all you've got. If he gets up, he'll be dangerous."

"That sounds like good advice."

"Or, alternatively, you could just leave his ex-wife alone, before he knows about you."

"Too late for that," Stone said. "He was waiting outside my house this morning when we left to go car shopping, and he followed us all the way to Bloomie's."

"What did you buy?"

"Not I, she. A Bentley Flying Spur. Is her check going to clear? I vouched for her."

"No problem there. Harry Hillman is a rich man—or was before he met Kitty."

"I can relax, then."

"I wouldn't do that, not with Harry on my tail."

"Noted. Any thoughts on how to discourage him?"

"I mentioned getting in the first punch, didn't I?"

"You did."

"After that, you're on your own. If you have a pair of brass knuckles tucked away, you might tuck them into a pocket."

"They ruin the line of a suit."

"Not as much as rolling around on the pavement."

"Point taken. See you soon."

"Bye."

They both hung up.

"Fred," Stone called out.

"Yes, sir?"

"Do you have some brass knuckles?"

"Not on me, sir, but just a moment." He rummaged in the armrest compartment, then handed Stone something: two rolls of quarters. "They'll have much the same effect as the knuckles, sir, but they're worse on the hands. You might think of wearing gloves. There are some in your seatback pocket."

"Right." Stone reached into the pocket, pulled out some fur-lined gloves, and slipped into them. "Is the Mercedes still with us, Fred?"

"He is, sir. Like he was bolted to our bumper."

"Pull over somewhere along here, and keep the engine running."

Fred pulled over. "You need some backup, sir?"

"You might keep an eye on his driver."

"Righto." Fred put the car in park, got out, and stood by his door.

The Mercedes passed, then pulled over in front of the Bentley. Harry Hillman got out, and he was, Stone reflected, as advertised. Stone leaned on the Bentley's rear door, crossed his arms, and waited.

"I'd like a word with you, my friend," Harry Hillman said and continued toward Stone without breaking his stride.

Stone pushed off the car and, grasping a roll of quarters in each hand, keeping his left side toward Hillman, waited another step, then hit the big man hard, with a straight left to the nose. Then, while Hillman took a moment to figure out why he was in pain and bleeding, Stone delivered a hard right to a spot just under the man's heart, which dropped him to one knee. Without hesitating, Stone swung a roundhouse right to his head, catching him under the ear.

Hillman lay on his back, gasping and staring at the sky. Out of the corner of his eye, Stone saw Hillman's driver start to step forward, when Fred, moving faster, stepped between Hillman and the driver. "Now, son," Fred said gently. "All you want to do is to get him up, into the car, and out of here with no further fuss."

The man stopped and nodded. Stone got back into the Bentley, and so did Fred. In a moment, it was all behind them.

"I don't think you'll have any more trouble with him, sir," Fred said.

"Not if I see him coming," Stone replied.

"Keep the quarters, just in case."

"Good idea."

"I've got a blackjack somewhere," Fred said. "You're welcome to that, too."

"A blackjack will get you put in jail in New York," Stone said. "Quarters are just pocket change."

"Well, there is that," Fred replied, then drove on.

S tone called Kitty on Monday morning. "Did you successfully
sack Bloomingdale's?"

"You might say that. I got a few things that will go nicely
with the car."

"I never thought of the car as a fashion accessory."

"The car is the object. The clothes are the accessories."

"Thank you for clearing that up for me."

"Anytime."

"I fear you may not have told me enough about your ex-
husband."

"What more could you possibly want to know? How he is
in bed?"

"No, what concerns me is how he is on the street, or rather, in
the gutter."

"Do you mean, is he a street fighter?"

"That's the idea. And, perhaps, if he enjoys it a little too much."

"Have you engaged with him in a street fight?"

"I'm afraid so."

"Are you calling from the emergency room?"

"No, but our boy, Harry, may be seeking solace there."

"You mean, you fought him and won?"

"Let's say I avoided losing, and he did not."

"My goodness, Stone, I have underestimated you."

"I'm sorry I came up short in your prior assessment."

"Not anymore."

"Perhaps you could render an opinion on whether Harry will come back for more."

"I'd say that is highly likely," she replied. "Especially if he lost. And next time, he'll be ready."

"I don't think you and I should see each other anymore."

"Heavens, Stone, how could I have been more cooperative?"

"It's not that. It's that I suspect you of encouraging a fight with Harry without telling me what to expect."

"Did that hurt your feelings, dear?"

"Not as much as it hurt Harry's."

"Well, let me tell you that I had no intention of bringing that about. I never thought Harry would be a problem for you, and I figured that, if he were, you could handle it, which you have. Besides, I so enjoyed you in bed. Harry is certainly no match for you there."

"Flattery might get you somewhere," Stone said. "I'll call you, after I've survived my next encounter with Harry." He hung up.

F ive minutes later, the phone rang again.

"Hello?"

"Stone, it's Viv."

"Hi, Viv. You know, you should rent out your matchmaking skills to the Heavyweight Division of the American Boxing Association."

"I heard about your tiff with Harry."

"'Tiff'? Ask Harry about that."

"I called him, but he wasn't picking up."

"And what had you planned to say to him?"

"I was going to upbraid him for picking a fight with Kitty's new boyfriend."

"Harry didn't pick the fight. I did."

"Oh, dear, did he hurt you?"

"Let's just say that he was slow getting up."

"You hurt Harry?"

"I showed him the view from the gutter, before he could show me."

"This is all my fault," Viv said.

"You may rightfully share the blame with Kitty."

"I've no problem with that," she said.

"You know, if I hadn't done a little research on Harry, I might be speaking to you now from a hospital bed, or perhaps even from a slab at the morgue. Either of you could have warned me, but nobody said anything."

"Research? What kind of research?"

"I spoke to a mutual acquaintance, with some knowledge of Harry's temperament."

"And who was that?"

"It was a confidential source and will remain so."

"Well, I apologize for whatever role I might have played."

"If you want to get back in my good graces, do it with information."

"What kind of information?"

"Well, at some point I imagine that Harry's ego is going to demand a rematch. I would like to know when that is."

"I'll do what I can, Stone. That's all I can do. Ear to the ground, I promise."

"I'd like to see that," Stone said, but Viv had already hung up. Stone's next call was to Dino.

"Bacchetti."

"It's Stone."

"Hi, there. I hear you and Harry Hillman did a little dancing."

"Harry did the dancing. I just kept him moving."

"You saw him coming, then?"

"Yes, and he didn't see me, until it was too late. Did you know about Harry's tendency toward violence?"

"There were times when there was a whiff of it in the air."

"The next time your nose knows, I'd like to hear about it."

"I'll keep that in mind. Did you incur any damage?"

"Well, my knuckles are a little sore."

"Did you have any weapons?"

"Fred loaned me a couple of rolls of quarters."

"That would add some weight to your punch."

"They achieved the desired effect."

"Do you think Harry is going to take it lying down?"

"Well, he was lying down when I last saw him, but I am reliably informed that when he figures out what happened he'll be back, and on his feet."

"And how are you preparing for that?"

"I don't know. Can you still buy an axe handle in this city?"

"Probably, but it's a little obvious. Doesn't conceal well. Don't you still have your old police baton?"

"Somewhere, I guess. I'll have to look around."

"Do it before you leave the house again."

"You haven't encouraged me to go armed. Why is that?"

"Shooting deaths are already up this year over last, and I wouldn't want you to add to the numbers."

"That's sweet of you."

"My advice on that front, if you decide to carry, is to use the .380, not the .45. The cleanup is easier."

"I'm not sure the .380 would stop him; he's something of an ox."

"A head shot with the .380 will drop him in his tracks. God, I hope nobody is listening to me telling you how to murder somebody."

"I believe we were discussing self-defense," Stone said.

"Of course we were. Dinner at Clarke's?"

"Six-thirty." They both hung up.

Stone went looking for his police baton.

12

Stone arrived at P.J. Clarke's on time, and the mob at the bar had thinned out just enough for him to grab a stool. The bartender saw him coming and got his Knob Creek on the bar just as he sat down. He had just taken his first sip when he glanced at his reflection in the mirror behind the bar and saw a very large person standing behind him. Stone unbuttoned his jacket for easier access to the baton.

"I want a word with you," an English accent said from behind him.

"Cat got your tongue?" Stone asked, without looking at him.

There was a kind of gargling noise.

"Speak up," Stone said.

"My name is Harry Hillman, and all I want from you is a fair fight."

"There's no such thing as a fair fight," Stone said. "You must be thinking of a boxing match, in a ring, with a referee."

"You've been tampering with my wife."

"You don't have a wife," Stone said. "The State of New York says so."

"Never mind her. This is between you and me."

"I believe we've already had that conversation," Stone said. "As far as I'm concerned, that settled anything between you and me, so take a hike."

Stone looked up and saw Dino step into the reflection, and he was holding up his badge. "Stand still," Dino said, frisking the larger man and coming up with a nine mm. "Do you have a license to carry this in the City of New York?"

"I certainly do," Hillman replied.

"Then let's see it."

"I don't have it on my person," Hillman said.

"Then you may consider this weapon confiscated, and unless you can present your carry license to the desk sergeant at the Nineteenth Precinct before nine AM tomorrow, you'll be confiscated, too. Now go away."

Hillman poked Stone hard in the back with a finger. "I'll speak to you later."

"I believe that constitutes battery. Can you arrest him, please, Officer?"

"I missed that," Dino said. He turned to Hillman. "Do it again, so I can arrest you."

Hillman had vanished from the reflection.

"Mr. Barrington," Dino said, "your table is ready."

Stone followed Dino into the dining room where they sat down and were given menus.

"So," Dino said. "Am I going to have to keep rescuing you from the clutches of the angry ex-husband?"

"Don't worry," Stone said. "I'm carrying a .380 and my trusty—make that rusty—telescopic baton, so I should be able to fend him off."

"Then stop turning your back on him."

"My back was there first. He sneaked up on me."

"I hate to think what's going to happen to you, if he connects with a punch."

"Let's talk about something else," Stone replied uncomfortably.

"Okay, let's talk about Kitty. What's her part in all this?"

"Innocent bystander," Stone said.

"There's nothing innocent about Kitty. I think she's trying to punish somebody, but I can't figure out if it's the ex or you."

"She has no reason to punish me," Stone said. "I've given her nothing but pleasure, by my reckoning. Don't mention that to the ex, if you meet him again."

"Did her check for the Bentley clear the bank?"

"I haven't had any calls from bank managers or the dealer, so I would assume so."

"Maybe the bank just deducted it from your account."

"I thought of that. Different banks."

"I guess you're in the clear, then."

They ordered another drink and some food, then Stone's phone rang. "Hello?"

"It's Kitty. How are you, my darling?"

"As well as can be expected," Stone replied.

"Uh-oh, have you had further, ah, contact with Harry?"

"He appeared, standing behind me at the bar at P.J. Clarke's a few minutes ago, but Dino waved his badge at him and scared him off."

"I'm so sorry about that. I thought that he would take my seeing somebody better than he has."

"I'm sorry you were disappointed," Stone said. "As things stand, this isn't going to end until one or both of us is mortally wounded, or worse."

"I'll have a word with Harry."

"It's going to take many words, I fear, and if you could slip in a mention of grievous bodily harm or even death, that might help."

"As you wish. Oh, the reason I called was to apologize about that cockup at the bank."

Stone's stomach made some sort of sideways movement. "Whose bank?"

"Mine. It seems that my broker didn't move the requested funds into my account quickly enough, and so my check has been returned to the dealer, unpaid."

Stone struggled for words.

"It sounds as if you're struggling for words," Kitty said.

"Ah, yes. So now, the dealer is coming after me to make your check good?"

"It won't come to that, sweetie," Kitty purred. "All will be made right tomorrow."

"Please say that you will make it so."

"Of course."

"I'd hate for the dealer to show up at your building, seeking the return of the car," Stone added for emphasis.

"Could they do that?"

"They could. Have another chat with your banker first thing tomorrow and ask them to see that the funds are available to cover your check."

"I'll do that very thing," Kitty said. "And I'll have that word—ah, words, with Harry."

"Thank you, Kitty. I have to eat a steak now. Goodbye." He hung up.

"You guaranteed her check for a Bentley?" Dino asked. "Really?"

"It wasn't like that. I just told the dealer that I would vouch for her."

"You're the lawyer. Doesn't that mean you'll cover her check?"

"Vouching is just expressing an opinion that she's good for it," Stone said.

"Would a judge buy that?"

"It won't go that far. Her broker was just slow at moving money to her checking account."

"It was what? A quarter of a million dollars?"

"Give or take."

"I can loan you a few thousand, but not the whole melon."

"There's no melon, Dino. The check will be paid tomorrow morning."

"Well, if you have to pay it, that will do wonders for your reputation."

"What do you mean?"

"I mean that the dealer, for one, will be very impressed that you made good on the check."

"None of that is going to happen, Dino. It was just a glitch."

"What if Harry kills Kitty before the check clears?"

"Harry wants to kill me, not Kitty."

"You never know when you're dealing with someone in that frame of mind. Will the check get paid if she's at the bottom of the East River?"

"Stop it."

"Well, maybe her banker doesn't read the tabloids or watch local TV news. I'm sure it will be fine."

"Thank you for your confidence."

"Of course, if . . ."

"Dino, if you say another word, I'm going to hit you with a steak."

Dino took a big bite of his steak and managed to chew and grin at the same time.

S tone had just tied his necktie and was about to go downstairs
    when his phone rang at the stroke of nine o'clock. "Hello?"
        "Mr. Barrington?"
    "Yes?"
    "It's Stephen, at Bentley. I'm afraid Ms. Crosse's check didn't
clear this morning."
    "Perhaps you should speak with her bank manager?"
    "I just spoke to him. She can't cover the check."
    "Please don't worry about it. It will happen this morning."
    "Oh, I'm not worried about it, Mr. Barrington. We've dealt with
you for some years, and I know we can expect you to do the right
thing."
    "What's the 'right thing'?" Stone asked.
    "Just wire transfer us the funds, and when Ms. Crosse's check
clears, we'll wire it right back to you."

"Well, ah . . ."

"You did say you vouched for her."

"Right, I did. Give me your wiring information." The man had it ready, and Stone wrote it down. "I'll wire it straightaway," Stone said. "Oh, what's the exact amount?"

"Let's call it an even $266,000. That car has a lot of options bolted onto it."

"Right. Sit by your phone."

"Don't worry, I'll be right here."

Stone hung up and called Joan.

"Yes, boss?"

"I'd like you to wire transfer some funds to the Bentley dealer right away. Got a pencil?"

"Ready."

Stone gave her the wiring information.

"What's the amount?"

"An even $266,000. Do we have that much in my account?"

"We do."

"And do it right now, please."

"Yes, sir, right away."

Stone went downstairs and settled in behind his desk. The phone rang. "Yes?"

"Stephen, from Bentley on one for you."

Stone picked up. "Yes, Stephen?"

"The funds arrived," the man said. "Don't worry, we'll get the sum right back to you as soon as we hear from Ms. Crosse's bank."

"Thank you, Stephen." He hung up and grabbed his coffee mug. At nine-thirty, Joan buzzed him. "Kitty Crosse on one for you. Is that a real person?"

"Yes, it is." He took a deep breath and pressed the button. "Yes, Kitty?"

"Oh, hello, Stone."

"I trust you've heard from your bank. I had to wire the dealer the funds to cover you."

"Oh, that was so sweet of you, Stone."

"Everything okay now?"

"Well, it should be."

"*Should* be?"

"I've been calling my broker, but they're not answering. The phone just rings and rings."

Stone frowned. "Who is your broker?"

"Viktor Zanian, with a *k*."

Stone clapped his hand over his mouth, so if he vomited, it wouldn't go all over his desk.

"How much do you have in your account there?" he managed to ask.

"Oh, several million. More than enough to cover the Bentley." He could hear a ringing noise in the background. "I'll have to call you back, Stone. My other line is ringing."

"Kitty . . ." But she had already hung up. Stone plucked a fistful of tissues from the box on his desk. He mopped his brow and took deep breaths to dispel the nausea. The phone rang. "Yes?"

"It's that Ms. Crosse again."

"Right." He pressed the button. "Yes, Kitty?"

"Oh, Stone, I've just had some awful news," she said. "A woman from the Zanian Fund just called and said that there was some sort of glitch, and they don't have access to my funds. What do you suppose that means?"

Stone took another deep breath. "It very likely means that your funds are in an offshore account somewhere—who knows where."

"Why would Mr. Zanian take my money offshore?"

"Kitty, do you read the newspapers or listen to the news on TV? Ever?"

"Well, hardly ever. What kind of question is that?"

"If you paid any attention at all, you wouldn't have to ask that question."

"Stone, do please try and make some sense."

"Sit down and listen to me, and I'll explain it to you. Viktor Zanian, when last seen by anyone, was getting off a private jet in Rio de Janeiro, Brazil, with several pieces of luggage."

"Well, when one travels, one takes luggage, doesn't one?"

"Yes, but Mr. Zanian's luggage contains all the funds you deposited with him, and those of many other unfortunate clients, as well. Mr. Zanian's offices have been padlocked by the U.S. government, and the FBI is looking for him, which is why no one is answering his phone."

"Stone, that is just not possible. Viktor Zanian is an upstanding gentleman."

"Mr. Zanian is neither upstanding, nor is he a gentleman, Kitty. He is a confidence man and a thief. Do you possess a computer?"

"Yes, of course."

"Do you know how to use Google?"

"Yes, do you think I'm some sort of dummy?"

"No, but Mr. Zanian does. Google him."

"I'll call you back."

Stone took the moment to remember that he could afford the loss he had just taken. That was of no comfort whatsoever.

Joan buzzed him.

"Is it Ms. Crosse?"

"How did you guess?"

Stone pressed the button. "Yes, Kitty?"

"Well, now I don't know whom to believe."

"What are the choices?" Stone asked.

"You or Google."

"Believe either. Google and I are not at odds."

"Well, Google has never lied to me," she said.

"Neither have I," Stone pointed out. "Kitty, you didn't deposit all your funds with Zanian, did you? I mean, you have other accounts. At your bank and, perhaps, at other institutions, for instance."

"Well, of course."

"I'm relieved to hear it," Stone replied. "Now, will you please wire transfer $266,000 to me immediately? My secretary will give you the account information."

"You mean the money I owe the Bentley people?"

"Exactly."

"Then I should wire it to them, shouldn't I?"

"I have already done so," Stone replied. "Now I would like you to reimburse me."

"What was the amount again?"

"It's $266,000."

"Oh, dear, I don't think I have that much in the bank at the moment."

"Then why did you write a check in that amount to the Bentley people?"

"Well, I *told* them I needed to move the money into my checking account. I don't believe there's that much in the account at the moment."

"How much is in the account?" Stone asked.

"Just a minute, I have a statement here somewhere." There was a rustling of papers, then the tearing of an envelope. "Here we are," she said. "Let's see. The current balance is $245.12."

"Is that after deducting the check to Bentley?"

"Oh, no, before."

"Oh, no."

"Stone, I *told* both you and the Bentley people that I had to move money to the account."

"Kitty, I need to think about our next move. I'll call you back later."

Stone hung up and pressed his forehead to the glass top on his desk.

S tone had just finished his lunch when the phone rang, and Joan was at lunch. He picked up. "This is Stone Barrington."

"Oh, I had hoped it would be," Kitty said. "I realized after our last conversation that I had forgotten to mention something important."

Stone managed not to groan. "What is it, Kitty?"

"I want to sue Viktor Zanian," she said.

"Kitty, *everybody* wants to sue Viktor Zanian."

"Not Mr. Zanian, exactly. I want to sue Harry."

"Your ex-husband?"

"Yes."

"Sue him for what?"

"Bad advice."

"What advice?"

"It was he who urged me to put all my money with Zanian."

"Well, you might have some sort of case, but you'll need to speak to your attorney about that."

"I want you to be my attorney."

"I'm afraid that would be unethical," Stone said.

"How would it be unethical? I need an attorney, you're an attorney."

"Yes, but the bar association frowns on attorneys who have, ah, a relationship with the client."

"Do you mean because we're fucking?"

"That's exactly what I mean."

"Well, that's very old-fashioned of them."

"I suppose it is. Why don't you talk to Herb?"

"Oh, he's just for divorces, and Harry and I are already divorced."

"No, Herb handles all sorts of legal cases. He's an excellent attorney, and I'm sure he would be happy to represent you in the matter."

"You're sure?"

"He's my law partner at Woodman & Weld. I'm sure."

"You know," she said, "when I mentioned that word—you know the one—I got a twinge, you know?"

"I think I do. I got a twinge, too."

"Sort of like an itch?"

"Very well put."

"Why don't we scratch that itch?" she asked.

"What a good idea. How about dinner at my house this evening?"

"Perfect. What time?"

"Drinks at six-thirty, scratching after dinner."

"See you then," she sang, and hung up.

Stone called Herbie Fisher.

"Herb Fisher."

"It's Stone. You're going to get a call from Kitty Crosse about suing her ex-husband."

"I thought he was about all sued out."

"She has a new grievance: old Harry persuaded her to invest all her money with Viktor Zanian."

"Does she have anything left?"

"She mentioned a figure of $245, give or take."

"You're sending me a penurious client? Thanks a lot."

"She's already your client. How much is Harry worth?"

"According to his financial statement submitted to the court, in excess of sixty million dollars."

"There you go," Stone said. "Perhaps, in light of events, you can reopen the settlement negotiations."

"Are you sure you don't want to handle this yourself?" Herb asked.

"You've already pointed out it would be unethical for me to do so."

"Have you stopped yet?"

"No."

"Oh, all right. I'll take her call."

Stone hung up and breathed a sigh of relief. He called Fred's wife, Helene, who was the cook and housekeeper, and ordered dinner for two in the study at seven o'clock.

The phone rang again. Stone hoped Kitty had not changed her mind. "Stone Barrington."

"Don't you have a secretary?" a man's voice said with a British accent.

"She's at lunch. Who is this?"

"It's Harry Hillman. I'd like to arrange an appointment with you."

"For what purpose?"

"I'd like to discuss you handling a legal matter for me. My ex-wife is suing me."

"Stop right there," Stone said. "I have no interest in representing you in any matter."

"It's because you're fucking her, isn't it?"

"Mr. Hillman, I have no interest in representing you."

"And I was going to apologize to you!"

"For what?" Stone asked.

"Well, I did treat you rather roughly, didn't I?"

"That's not the way I remember it," Stone said.

"I mean at the bar at Clarke's. That poke in the back I gave you. I apologize for doing that."

"Apology accepted. Good day." Stone hung up.

Joan came into his office. "Anything new?" she asked.

"Nothing whatever. If a person named Harry Hillman calls, on no account put him through to me. You can say that I do not wish to speak to him."

"I understand. It's the ex-husband, isn't it?"

"It is."

"Lordy, how I wish you would stay away from women with ex-husbands."

"You want me to take up celibacy? Virtually every attractive

71

woman over thirty in the city has at least one ex-husband. They're a standard liability, and not all of them are violent or crazy or both."

"It just seems that way, I suppose," Joan replied. "Okay, no calls from a Mr. Harry Hillman. How about Mrs. Hillman?"

"The former Mrs. Hillman. I believe you're referring to Ms. Crosse."

"Ah, that I am."

"Her calls are welcome."

"Understood."

Stone spent a little time tidying up his study and opened the folding table, so that Fred could set it. When it was all done, he went upstairs to shower and change, considering his wardrobe along the way. It didn't seem necessary to wear a jacket, underwear, or socks; they would just be impediments. He buttoned every other button on his shirt.

Kitty was only a few minutes late, and it was immediately apparent to Stone that she had made wardrobe choices that very much followed his thinking: a pretty dress, short with straps, no underthings that he could detect. He fixed them drinks.

"Oh," Kitty said, taking an envelope from her purse. "I have a little present for you."

He handed over her martini, and they toasted each other, then sat down. Stone opened the envelope and found that it contained a cashier's check from her bank, made out to him in the amount of $266,000. "Oh," he said, placing a hand on his chest, "that makes my heart go pittypat."

"Herb Fisher called this afternoon to say that his office had received the final payment from Harry for our divorce settlement, which was wired to his firm's account. It was a little over seven million dollars. I had quite forgotten about it. Herb asked me to give you the news."

"My God," Stone said. "A woman who can forget she has a seven-million-dollar payment coming! You are extraordinary!"

"Just a little untidy about financial matters."

They had a second drink before dinner, which was veal scallopini. Stone felt that something light would be best.

After dinner they went to the master suite, Stone following Kitty up the stairs. The view was marvelous, he thought.

Kitty pushed the straps off her shoulders, and her dress collapsed around her ankles, revealing all. Stone was nearly as fast, kicking his trousers across the room. She pushed him onto the bed and stroked him erect, then did wonderful things with her lips and tongue. Stone reciprocated.

They made love slowly, drawing out the orgasm to its maximum extent before letting go.

"That was everything I remember from before," she said, cradling his head in her lap and stroking his hair.

"Same here," he said. After a little rest, he took two dishes of ice cream from the freezer in his little fridge. "I thought we'd have dessert after dessert," he said.

"Yum," she said. "What is it?"

"Macadamia brittle," he replied. "My favorite.

"Stone," she said, setting aside her bowl, "have you ever had fellatio from someone who's been eating ice cream?"

"I can't say that I have," Stone replied.

"Hang on," she said, bending to her task.

Stone made appreciative noises, with no effort at all.

15

Viv was traveling again, so Stone and Dino had dinner at Café Un Deux Trois, a brasserie on West Forty-Fourth Street, the sort of traditional French restaurant that specialized in Steak Frites, a steak with French fries. The best bottle of wine on the *carte du vins* wasn't expensive, so they ordered that.

"What's new on the Kitty front?" Dino asked.

"She has, amazingly, repaid her debt to me for the car."

"How many rolls in the hay did that take?"

"You defame her. She repaid last night with a cashier's check."

"My apologies to the lady. You wouldn't be walking and talking if she had worked it off."

"Crudely put, but not inaccurate," Stone said.

"What's she like in the sack?" Dino asked. When Stone frowned and shook his head, Dino said, "After all, she told Viv what you are like."

"That's right, she did. Does that relieve me of confidentiality regarding her charms?"

"I think the bar association would buy that," Dino said.

"All right, she is, in a word, spectacular."

"I guess that about covers it."

"I guess it does."

"Where'd she get the money to repay you with a cashier's check?"

"She forgot that her ex's final payment on her divorce settlement was due, and he coughed up on schedule."

"Coughed up how much?"

"Since she's not my client, I guess I can tell you: upward of seven mil."

"Wow!"

"I am reliably informed that ol' Harry is worth north of sixty mil, so it wasn't a strain for him."

"How does an Englishman get to be worth sixty mil?" Dino asked.

"The old-fashioned way: he inherited it. I'm assuming that, since he has no visible means of support—certainly not from Kitty, who got scalped for more than three mil by Zanian."

"Speaking of Zanian, I heard a rumor today."

"Lay it on me."

"I stress that it's just a rumor. I have no evidence to back it up."

"Tell me anyway, just for the fun of it."

"There are those who say that our boy Viktor isn't in Rio at all, that he never left the States."

"And the film of him getting off the plane in Rio?"

"Staged."

"How substantial a rumor is this?"

"On what scale?"

"Zero to ten—ten is irrefutable."

"Maybe a four."

"That substantial? Really?"

"The guy I heard it from is not usually given to fantasy."

"And it's on that basis alone that you rate the rumor a four?"

"If I didn't think it could be true, I would have given it a zero, or maybe a one."

"That's interesting. Does the rumor contain a location?"

"He could still be in New York City."

"And you find that plausible?"

"Wouldn't you?" Dino asked. "If he were in Rio, this is the last place anybody would look for him."

"Have you got people on this?"

"Nah, it's a federal case. We couldn't care less."

"Except to start rumors. Is it a federal rumor or local?"

"It's federal."

"Do you give more weight to federal rumors than local ones?"

"Well, if it was local, I'd expect more backup."

"I see. So, how would somebody fake the Rio film?"

"Are you kidding? Haven't you seen any movies lately? They can make anything appear to be anything else. I saw one the other night that made the White House explode. They can do that, they can put Zanian in Rio, no problem."

"You have a point," Stone said.

"Of course, you no longer have an interest in Zanian, because you got your money back."

"I didn't get it back from Zanian, so he's fair game. Is there a reward for the guy?"

"There's a rumor that somebody has come up with ten million bucks for arrest and conviction, but it hasn't been posted yet."

"Maybe not," Stone said, "but your rumors are getting more interesting."

"I thought that, too. I'd rate this one as an eight."

"Now *that's* interesting."

"To find out if it's true, all you have to do is wait until tomorrow. That's when they're supposed to make the announcement."

"I'll try and be patient."

"And, of course, you still have a personal interest in seeing Zanian caught."

"Ah, yes," Stone said. "Tink."

"I take it she has not been visiting you since Zanian ran off with her money."

"You take it correctly. She was even behaving as if it were my fault, even though I warned her off—even put it in writing."

"Some people resent it when people who give them dire warnings turn out to be right."

"They do, don't they? You'd think they'd be more appreciative, wouldn't you?"

"Nah, they resent being told, 'I told you so.'"

"You're rich enough to cover her loss," Dino said. "That would secure you a warmer place in her, ah, heart."

Stone shook his head. "No, it would be like paying for sex. I'd rather preserve my amateur standing."

"You've never paid for sex?"

"Well, once, in college when it seemed to be the only way I'd ever get laid. Since then, my record is right up to Olympic standards."

"Well, I hope, for your sake, that Tink gets her money back and gives you credit for it."

"I don't see that happening, do you?"

"Nah," Dino said. "It's not how women think."

"That's a sexist remark," Stone said.

"I don't care. My wife's not listening."

16

The following morning Stone called Bob Cantor, who was his go-to tech guy for just about everything.

"What's up, Stone?"

"Hey, Bob. Have you been following the Viktor Zanian story?"

"Just when it comes on the news."

"Did you see the shot of him getting off his Gulfstream in Rio?"

"Yeah, I did."

"Did you notice anything odd about it?"

"Funny you should mention that," Bob said. "I thought it looked a little hinky."

"Can you take a closer look at it and see if it could have been taken somewhere else?"

"Okay, I'll have to dig up a copy of the film or tape. Let me call you back later."

"Great!"

Stone hung up and went back to doing what passed for work. Just before lunch, Joan buzzed him.

"Are you taking calls from Tink Dorsey?"

"Sure," Stone said, pressing a button. "Hello, Tink."

"Hi, Stone. Are you speaking to me?"

"I never stopped."

"I know, I know. It was me. I screwed things up."

"Don't be too hard on yourself. You had just had a very bad shock."

"I read your letter again. It was exactly what a good friend would say to me, and it's my fault for not paying attention to it. It's all on me."

"Have you heard anything encouraging about Zanian?"

"Just form letters from the SEC."

"You signed up with them?"

"I did. Who knows? I might see some of my money again someday."

"I hope so."

"Have you, ah, missed me?"

"Can you be more specific?" he asked, teasing.

"All right, have you missed the fucking? I know I have."

"I have."

"Why don't we see what we can do about that?"

"Well . . . as nice an idea as that is, I've told you I've been seeing somebody."

"Where'd you meet her?"

"A blind date."

"You think blind girls are a turn-on? That's sick!"

"You know what I mean."

"Is she as good as me in bed?"

"Comparisons are odious."

"I'm prepared to overlook the presence of another woman in your life."

"That's generous of you, but I'm not sure she would share your generosity."

"You mean share you?"

"Well, yes, and I don't want to raise the subject. It would make me sound greedy."

"You *are* greedy."

"Well, under some circumstances, I suppose so."

"Tell you what, let's leave the offer open. You never can tell."

"No, you can't, can you? Let's do that."

"Bye-bye."

"Bye." Stone hung up wondering if he had done the right thing. Then he realized what had been worrying him. Did he have the stamina to keep up with both of them? Probably not, he conceded to himself. That could lead to an early death.

After lunch, Joan buzzed. "Bob Cantor is here. Do you want to see him?"

"Yes, please. Send him in."

Bob walked in carrying a laptop. "I've got something for you," he said, setting his laptop on Stone's desk and turning it on. "Look, here's the shot of Zanian getting off the airplane in Rio. It's shot from inside his airplane, over his shoulder. And the view is Landmark Aviation, Rio de Janeiro, as it says on the building ahead of him, right?"

"Right," Stone replied.

"Wrong," Bob said. He tapped a few more keys. "Look familiar?"

Stone looked at the shot. Everything was the same, except the building he could see had Jet Aviation, Teterboro, written on it. "That's where I keep my airplane," Stone said.

"I thought you'd recognize it." Bob tapped some more keys, and the Rio shot came up again.

"I did some checking on the FAA website. On the day Zanian took a powder, his airplane filed a flight plan to Rio."

"Did they cancel later?"

"No, the airplane actually flew to Rio and landed. The mani-fest listed only Viktor Zanian and a Ms. Shelly Summers. I ran her name and she worked at an expensive escort service, called Com-pany On Call, and she quit the day before the feds clamped down on Zanian's business."

"And she went along for the ride to Rio?"

"No, neither of them did. There were two other people who took the ride, and came back with the airplane to Teterboro."

"So, Zanian had all the time it took for the airplane to reach Rio to get lost somewhere else."

"And five'll get you ten, the airplane was sold the next day to a Delaware corporation."

"You check on that. Let's be sure."

"And we'll see, too, if the airplane has flown anywhere since the transfer. I've signed up his tail number with an online service that will alert me whenever they file a flight plan."

"Question, Bob: If you can figure this out in a day, have the feds figured it out, too?"

"I can ask around, but they may be sitting tight on that info. Why don't you ask Dino to take a look at it, too? Cops don't like the feds. They like to see them embarrassed."

"Good idea. You stay on where the airplane has gone, and who's flying on it."

"I can do that," Bob said.

S tone called Dino.

"Bacchetti."

"I haven't heard the announcement from the FBI about the reward for Viktor Zanian. Is that still on?"

"Far as I know. I . . . Hang on." There was a brief pause. "It's on CNN now."

"Hang on." Stone switched on the TV. He got the last of the announcement and jotted down the phone number. "Got it."

"Do I get half?" Dino asked. "I'm the one who gave you the tip."

Stone didn't have to think about it. "Yes, you get half, but you have to work for it."

"'Work'? What does that mean?"

"I know you are only fleetingly acquainted with the concept, so let's get started. Who's running the case at the Bureau?"

"Brio Ness," Dino replied without hesitation.

"Is that a boy Brio or a girl Brio?"

"Female. I'm not allowed to say 'girl' at the office. She reports directly to the director."

"That cuts a lot of red tape, doesn't it?"

"It also allows the director to take a lot of the credit, when they put the cuffs on Zanian."

"Of course it does. I've got more info coming on the possible whereabouts of Zanian. I'll call Ms. Ness when I have that."

"Up to you, pal, just don't mention my name in connection with the reward. As far as she's concerned, you're getting the whole sausage." He gave Stone her direct line.

"Gotcha. Dinner later?"

"Viv has booked us for seven o'clock at the Carlyle. Bring Kitty, Viv would like that."

"Will do." Stone hung up and was immediately buzzed by Joan. "Bob Cantor holding on two."

Stone pressed the button. "Yeah, Bob."

"You'll like this: Zanian's Gulfstream changed destinations and landed at Waterbury-Oxford Airport, in Connecticut. This morning it departed for Aspen with two passengers on board, a Mr. and Mrs. Taylor."

"Okay, good news. Who's the corporate owner of the airplane?"

"The Woodchip Corporation, of Wilmington, Delaware."

"Okay, keep me posted." Stone hung up and called Brio Ness's number.

"Special Agent Ness," a smooth voice said.

"Agent Ness, my name is Stone Barrington. I'm an attorney with Woodman & Weld."

"I've heard your name from Bill Eggers," she said. "What can I do for you?"

"Are you accepting hot leads on Viktor Zanian?"

"With both hands," she replied. "Whaddaya got?"

"Zanian didn't fly to Rio, but his airplane did, then it turned around and flew north again, filed for Teterboro, then redirected to Waterbury-Oxford Airport, Connecticut. The airplane's ownership was changed to a Delaware company, the Woodchip Corporation."

"Very interesting. What evidence do you have that Zanian didn't get off in Rio?"

"He wasn't on board. If you put your tech people on the film of him landing there, they will learn that it's faked. The film was shot at Teterboro, then doctored."

"And where is Mr. Zanian now?"

"His airplane left Oxford this morning, filed for Aspen. That's all I've got for the moment."

"Well, that's quite a lot, if any of it is true."

"I have every confidence that all of it is."

"I don't suppose you have any interest in the ten-million-dollar reward."

"On the contrary, I'm very much interested in it. I would appreciate a text from you, confirming the details that I gave you."

"Okay, Mr. Barrington, your information is noted, and you are now standing in line for the money."

"How far back in the line?"

"Pretty far, but I'll tell you this: your information is more inter-esting than anything I've heard so far. Now, you must excuse me while I get the wheels of justice turning."

"You are excused," Stone said. He hung up.

Stone called Kitty. "Are you awake?" he asked.

"Fairly," she said.

"How about dinner with the Bacchettis at the Carlyle, at seven?"

"I'll meet you there. It's just around the corner."

"See you then."

Stone was early, so he dropped into Bemelmans Bar for a drink. The little jazz group was just warming up, and he enjoyed lis-tening. The bartender, momentarily idle, walked over to Stone. "Your name Barrington?"

"That's right."

"Friend of mine says you're working on getting peoples' money back who invested with a guy named Zanian. That so?"

"Not really. I know a couple of people who lost some money, but the FBI is doing all the investigating. Did he take some of your money?"

"Friend of mine lost a bundle."

"How much is a bundle?"

"Three hundred grand."

"Who's your friend?"

"I don't want to say."

"What do you want to say?"

"Forget it. I was just curious."

"The FBI is offering a ten mil reward, you know."

The bartender brightened. "I heard."

"If you know anything about where Zanian is, they're the people to talk to."

"Well, you never know. You hear a lot of stuff tending bar at a place like this," the man said.

"What's your name?"

"Tim Deal."

"Good luck, Tim." He put some money on the bar and walked across the hall to the dining room where the Bacchettis awaited.

"You were in the bar, weren't you?" Dino asked.

"I was early and thirsty." They all ordered drinks and looked at the menu.

"Strange. Just now the bartender knew my name and asked me if I was working for some of Zanian's victims."

"Then you must be famous," Viv said.

"I know two people who lost money to Zanian. One of them is coming through the door right now." He nodded toward Kitty, who spotted them and headed for the table. Stone and Dino rose to meet her, and air was kissed.

"We were just talking about Zanian," Viv said.

"Everybody's talking about him," Kitty replied. "I had a phone call from somebody I didn't know, asking if I'd like them to get my money back."

"That's a scam," Stone said. "Next time, just hang up on them."

"How much did they want?" Dino asked.

"Ten thousand now and ten percent of what they recover."

"Yeah, it's a scam artist. They'll be coming out of the wood-work with ten million out there."

"How would he know my name?" Kitty asked.

"Has it been in the papers?"

"Not that I know of."

"Kitty," Stone said, "you don't read the papers. You could have been a headline in the *Post*, and you wouldn't know."

"True."

"I just had a bartender ask me if I was trying to get peoples' money back from Zanian."

"Did he know you?"

"He'd heard of me. His name is Tim Deal."

"Looks like we're all getting famous," Kitty said. "What did you say to Tim?"

"I told him if he knew anything to call the FBI."

They ordered, and Kitty, who was sitting next to Stone on the banquette, put her hand on his thigh and whispered, "My place is just around the corner. Later?"

"As soon as possible," Stone whispered back.

"I know what that was about," Viv said. "You two are embar-rassing us."

"I'm not embarrassed," Dino said.

18

Stone followed Kitty into her apartment, which was spacious, elegantly designed and decorated, and dimly lit.

"Bedroom is this way," Kitty said, a little breathlessly.

Two minutes later they were stretched out next to each other, caressing body parts.

"This is better than dessert," Kitty said.

Stone moved down her body to the delta. "This is dessert," he said, exploring.

"You're right," she said, opening up and pulling him into her by his hair. "Don't ever get a haircut," she said. "This is so convenient." She suddenly came, and he moved on to other places.

Kitty rolled him over. "Your turn to be dessert," she said.

They spent an hour pleasuring each other then fell asleep, entwined.

The following morning, Kitty threw on some clothes and left the apartment for a few minutes, returning with freshly baked croissants and other pastries. She made a pot of coffee, poured some freshly squeezed orange juice into a pitcher, and brought it all to the bed where Stone was sitting up, waiting.

"I had a call on my cell phone while I was standing in line at the bakery," she said. "An acquaintance of mine asked me if it is true that you are trying to get my money back from Zanian."

"I'm hearing a lot of that, and it isn't true. What did you tell your friend?"

"That I know you, but the rumor is not true."

"Thank you for that. Another hundred people would have heard it by lunchtime. I've never experienced anything quite like this."

"Perhaps some fame would be good for your practice."

"Not rumor fame. It just eats up time that should be billing at a thousand dollars an hour."

"Is that what you get?"

"It's what all the senior partners at Woodman & Weld get."

"Is Herb Fisher a senior partner?" she asked.

"Not yet. Soon, though."

"Oh, good. Why are you such a good lover?" she asked.

"Not I, you. You bring it out in me."

"You are kind."

"I am truthful, and the truth is not always kind." He looked at the bedside clock. "The truth is, I'd better be going. I have to shower and change before work."

"I don't want you to go, but I understand." She kissed him tenderly in a nice place.

S tone was back at his desk to take a call from Bob Cantor. "What are you hearing?"

"I'm hearing how you're going to get everybody's money back."

"From whom are you hearing that?"

"From everybody I talk to."

Stone looked at the stack of phone messages Joan had left on his desk. "It's infesting my workspace, too. Anything new to report?"

"Zanian's Gulfstream is still at Aspen, and it's snowing out there, so I expect they'll be grounded for a day or two."

"Thanks, gotta run." He hung up and buzzed Joan. She walked in. "What am I to do about all these calls from Zanian victims and the press on that subject?"

"Tell them each the same thing: that while I am acquainted with a couple of victims, I am not seeking to recover funds for anyone. Refer them to the FBI."

"Okay."

"And sound convincing."

"Okay, I'll try."

"You know how to sound convincing when you want to."

She closed the door behind her. The line continued to ring all morning, and Stone shut off the bell. Just before lunch, Joan announced that Bill Eggers, the managing partner of Woodman & Weld, was on the phone.

Stone picked it up. "Good morning, Bill. And no, I have not

found, nor am I searching for, the treasure of Viktor Zanian. I don't know how that rumor got started."

"I suspected you weren't," Eggers said. "Are you searching for the reward on Zanian?"

"That's different, but I'm not having any success."

"So, you are going after the reward?"

"Who in his right mind, if Zanian fell into his lap, would not welcome him and turn his ass in to the FBI?"

"But your lap is empty?"

"Would that it was not so."

"My wife has a friend who had a few million with Zanian," Eggers said.

"My condolences to her. Refer her to Herbie Fisher. He has a lot of spare energy for that sort of thing."

"Not a bad idea."

"Success would catapult him into a senior partnership, would it not?"

"If we got to keep the reward, sure."

"Tell him that, and he'll make the search his first priority."

"Okay, I'll do that right now."

"Thank you, Bill, and discourage rumormongers, will you? I don't have the time."

They both hung up. The light on the incoming line continued to flash every minute or two.

19

S tone was wrapping up for the day when Joan buzzed that
Bob Cantor was on the line.

"Put him through," Stone said.

"Stone? I'm glad I caught you."

"What's up, Bob?"

"I had a sneaking feeling about Zanian's airplane, so I called all
the FBOs in Aspen and found the one he was using. The manager
told me they refueled and took off just as the snow was starting."

"Bound for where?"

"I checked the records, and they filed for San Jose, California."

"That's interesting," Stone said, "but I don't know why."

"Most private jets headed for the West Coast are going to file
for Oakland, if they're going to San Francisco, or to one of the L.A.
area airports."

"Yeah, that makes sense. So, what reason would an aircraft's pilot have for filing for San Jose?"

"Well, San Jose is the last refueling you would have if you were headed for the Pacific."

"Where in the Pacific?"

"Gotta be Hawaii. You couldn't make Midway or Manila without a fuel stop."

"So, you're telling me that Zanian could be headed for anywhere in the world's largest ocean?"

"As long as he keeps refueling. I mean, the Gulfstreams are perfect airplanes for the long-distance stuff, but they drink Jet A, just like everything else."

"What else of interest is in San Jose?" Stone asked.

"Silicon Valley?"

"So where do you think Zanian is taking off for?"

"We won't know that until he takes off."

"Stay on this, Bob, and let me know that destination."

"Okay."

Stone thought about it for a minute, then called Brio Ness.

"Well, hello there," she said. "Have you called to claim the reward?"

"Not just yet," Stone replied, "but I'm working on it."

"Tell me about your work."

"Well, Zanian's airplane took off for Aspen."

"We looked into it and you were right. Didn't he get snowed in?"

"Wrong. They took off again before the snow became unmanageable, filed for San Jose, California."

"What would Zanian want in San Jose?"

"Fuel for Hawaii," Stone said. "He's headed for somewhere in the Pacific, but he'd have to refuel in Hawaii to make any of the other island destinations."

"Which airport in Hawaii?"

"We won't know that until he files his flight plan."

"You mean, the airplane hasn't left San Jose?"

"Not as of a few minutes ago."

"I'll scramble a team," she said. "Either we'll pick him up in San Jose or in Hawaii."

"Yeah, but at which Hawaiian airport? There's Oahu, the Big Island, Maui, maybe Hilo, probably more. Take your pick!"

"I can't cover half a dozen airports with the manpower we've got in the islands."

"Well, if I were flying the airplane, I'd file for some place like Oahu, then half an hour out of there, I'd call air traffic control and change my destination to another airport, say Hilo."

"You're a big help."

"I'm doing the best I can. Is anybody else doing better?"

"You have a point. I'd better call a raid on San Jose right now."

"Remember, there will be half a dozen FBOs there."

"What's an FBO?"

"A fixed-base operator. A filling station to you."

"How do I find out which one they're at?"

"I believe a gentleman named Bell invented the telephone some time ago. Surely the FBI has got enough nickels."

"I'll get right on it," she said, then hung up.

Stone was locking his desk when Cantor called again. "Hang on to your hat," he said. "They've filed for Hilo, and they're starting engines."

"Any guesses on where from Hilo?"

"Hilo's the closest airport to the U.S., but I don't think he's going there. I mean, who goes to Hilo for anything but fuel? He's got plenty of range for any airport in the islands."

"Where would he go from there?"

"Midway, Manila, Christmas Island?"

"Christmas Island? What the hell for?"

"Fuel for Australia. It's on the route."

"Oh, shit. I'd better warn the feds." He hung up and called Brio.

"Now what? The airplane is at Landmark Aviation. Two SWAT teams are suiting up."

"Hold on. The Gulfstream has filed for Hilo. They'll be gone before your people get there."

"What am I going to tell two SWAT teams?"

"Tell them to unsuit, and better luck next time."

"Shit!" she said. "God, I could use a drink."

"When do you get off?"

"That's a leading question, but I finished work five minutes ago."

"Where are you staying?"

"Upper East Side."

"Stop by my house for a drink, then."

"Let me get everybody to stand down, then I'll see you about six."

He gave her the address.

"Turtle Bay. I've always wondered about that neighborhood."

"All will be revealed," Stone said. "We'll see how you feel about dinner after your first drink."

"You're pushing your luck, but I'll see you at six." She hung up.

Cantor called back. "They've taken off," he said. "Eight people and a dog aboard."

"Six of those will be two flight crews and two attendants. They're geared up for long-haul flights, and the crew has to sleep sometime."

"Sounds that way."

"Call me on the cell when you're sure where they're landing."

"Okay."

Stone called Helene to see what kind of dinner she could put together on short notice.

20

Stone's doorbell rang at six-thirty. He pressed the intercom button. "Is that the FBI?"

"It is. Sorry I'm late."

"Come straight ahead, I'll meet you." He pressed the button that opened the door and walked into the living room. He had just a moment to size her up, and the report was favorable. "I'm Stone Barrington." He offered his hand.

She took it. "I'm Brio Ness. It's a nice hand, but why doesn't it have a drink in it?"

"I'll lead you to the watering hole," Stone said, walking her to the study.

"Nice living room," she said, while passing through. "Nice study," she said, when they had arrived.

"Thank you. We make a nice drink, too. What would you like?"

"A single malt Scotch on the rocks. It's been that kind of day."

"Laphroaig?"

"Whatever perfect is in Gaelic."

He poured and handed her a thick Baccarat whiskey glass, then poured himself a Knob Creek and waved her to the sofa.

"Ahhhh," she said, sinking in. "Your friend Zanian is getting me down."

"We're not friends. We've never met."

"What shall I call him, your meal ticket?"

"I eat quite well without his help. Call him my quarry."

"Done. God, this is wonderful Scotch."

"I tend to agree, but I'm a drinker of bourbon, by habit."

"I can't stay for dinner," she said.

"Of course, you can. I've already ordered, and it will be served shortly."

"Well, since you put it that way." She emptied her glass.

"There's time for one more before dinner," he said, repairing the damage.

"I just don't want you to think that I'm that kind of girl," she said.

"The kind who eats?"

"I don't do that on a first date."

"Eat? I recommend it three times daily."

Fred appeared at the door with a dusty bottle of wine in his hand. Stone introduced him to Brio. "Will this do for dinner, sir?"

"What are we having?"

"Porterhouse steak."

"That will do very nicely with beef. Please decant it, and a char- donnay with our first course."

Fred disappeared.

"You have a butler?"

"We call him a factotum. He's so much more than a butler: drives, decants, shoots bad people."

"You get a lot of those in the house?"

"They turn up now and then. Fred was the national pistol champion of the Royal Navy, two years running. He was a Marine."

"Pretty small for a Marine," she said.

"He beats up larger opponents all the time."

"I suppose that's handy, if you're in the wrong neighborhood."

"It is. I don't have the Federal Bureau of Investigation at my disposal. How did you make a career in the Bureau?"

"I figured out my last year in law school that I didn't want to practice law, and it seemed an interesting refuge."

"How long ago was that?"

"Nine years."

"Are you satisfied with your career progress?"

"No, but they wouldn't want me if I were. I'm doing okay."

"Reporting directly to the director on the Zanian thing."

"Once in a while something turns up that interests the higher-ups, but they don't want to do the work, of course."

"You do the work, and they take the credit, right?"

"Fairly right. I'll get a notation in my record if I make them look good enough."

"What, no decorations?"

"On rare occasions."

Fred reappeared with the wines. "Dinner is served, sir."

They started with a thick slice of smoked salmon, and a glass of a good Meursault. "The salmon is for the Scot in you," Stone explained.

"And how did you come into all this?" she asked, waving a fork.

"I had the same feeling as you did about the practice of law," Stone said. "So, I chose the NYPD and did fourteen years before they released me into the wild, working homicide the last few years."

"Well," she said, "maybe someone will murder Zanian, and you can put your old skills to work."

"From what I'm hearing," Stone said, "they're waiting in line to do just that, once they've got their money back."

"Not much chance of that, is there?"

"Is that what you're telling the director?"

"No, but that's what he believes. So, if I lay my hands on the guy, he'll be thrilled, never mind the money."

"The last big Ponzi guy was arrested in his office," Stone said. "Zanian was better prepared, his Gulfstream at the ready."

"My people are canvassing the Hawaiian airports," she said.

The porterhouse arrived, beautifully sliced, with a baked potato and asparagus. Fred poured the red for tasting, and Stone approved, so Brio got some, too.

They had an apple tart for dessert, with a glass of port from a decanter, then they repaired to the sofa.

"Now," Stone said, "we were discussing the kind of girl you're not."

"I'm reassessing my position on that," she replied. "You've gone to such lengths. Perhaps another time, when Zanian has not tired me out so."

"I understand," Stone said.

"Also, I think that will have to wait until Mr. Zanian sees the inside of a federal detention center, and the money for that reward has been distributed. It wouldn't look good for me to be associated with the collector of the money."

"Good thinking."

Fred drove her home in the Bentley.

21

Stone was having breakfast when Bob Cantor called.

"Yes, Bob?"

"Sorry it's so early, but I thought you'd want to know that Zanian's Gulfstream is down at San Jose. They're having to replace the auxilliary power unit."

"Good, that will slow him down for the FBI."

"The FBI has already raided the FBO: Zanian was not there, and neither were his pilots, and they were unable to connect the aircraft with him. They'll sit on the airplane until Zanian shows up and tries to fly away."

"How long before the unit can be replaced?"

"Late this afternoon eastern time."

Stone thought for a moment. "I want to be there," he said. "You want to go?"

"To San Jose? I've got no business there."

"How about Hawaii?"

"No time. Too much work."

"I'll let you know how it turns out."

Stone hung up and called his pilot, Faith. "We're headed for San Jose, California, ASAP," he said.

"Okay, boss."

"We may go as far as Hawaii. Put together a long-distance crew."

"Will do."

"What time can we take off?"

"With luck, eleven AM, if the right crew is available on short notice."

"I'll be there for wheels up at eleven. Let me know if there's any delay."

"Right."

Stone hung up and called Dino.

"Bacchetti."

"You want to have some fun?"

"How much fun?"

Stone explained the situation.

"That sounds like a *lot* of fun—and possibly profitable, too! See you at ten forty-five."

"Bring tropical clothing."

"I've got a Panama hat somewhere." Dino hung up.

Stone showered, shaved, dressed, and packed a couple of bags. When they arrived at the airport, Stone was amused to find that Faith had assembled an all-female crew, three pilots and two flight attendants.

They set down at San Jose at midafternoon and taxied to Landmark Aviation. While Faith ordered fuel, Stone and Dino went inside and found the manager.

"How can I help you?" the man asked.

"You have a Gulfstream in your shop to change the auxiliary power unit, don't you?" Stone asked.

"We did. It took off late this morning."

"Didn't you have a visit from the FBI?"

"We did, but the airplane was already gone."

"Gone where?"

"I'm not sure where they filed for. Check with the tower."

"How did you turn it around so fast?"

"We discovered that the unit was fine. The problem was a relay, and that was easily replaced."

"Thank you," Stone said. "Could you ask the tower where they filed for?"

"Sure." The man picked up a phone, spoke to somebody, and hung up. "Acapulco, Mexico."

"Thank you," Stone said.

"So, we're going to Acapulco?" Dino asked.

"Not yet," Stone said. He found Faith signing for the fuel. "Faith, will you go up to the tower and speak to the duty officer? Our Gulfstream filed for Acapulco this morning and took off, but I want to know if they've changed their destination, and if so, to where."

"Sure," Faith said, then left the airplane.

"Why didn't you ask the FBO manager to find out?"

"Faith is prettier," Stone replied. "She gets information out of people who didn't know they were going to give it to her."

Faith was back shortly. "They changed their destination to Hilo, Hawaii."

"File for Hilo, and let's get out of here. When we're an hour out, ask ATC if they changed their destination again."

"What do you think Zanian is doing for passports?" Dino asked, as they taxied to the runway.

"You don't need passports for Hawaii," Stone said, "but I'm sure he took care of the passport problem a long time ago. He certainly took care of everything else."

"Are you going to let the FBI know about this?"

"I've already done my duty in that regard," Stone said. "As far as I'm concerned, they're on their own now."

"Did you impart that to Brio Ness personally?"

"I did. She told me she was no longer interested in speaking to me about the matter of Zanian, and I'm going to take her at her word."

"What else did she tell you?"

"She told me that the Honolulu AOC doesn't have enough agents to cover all the Hawaiian airports, so maybe we'll get lucky."

"I know a guy who might be helpful when we get there," Dino said.

"We'll take all the help we can get," Stone said. "Right now, let's get some sleep."

22

Stone was wakened from a sound sleep by Faith, who was standing over him and talking.

"What?" he muttered.

"They've diverted to Honolulu. Shall I follow?"

"Yes. But check again with ATC to make sure they haven't changed airports again. And when we're down, ask which FBO the previous Gulfstream went to and go there."

"Will do," Faith said, then returned to the cockpit.

An hour later they touched down and rolled out, then Faith taxied to Signature Aviation. Stone went forward to speak to her. "Ask the FBO which hotel the other Gulfstream crew were booked into, then book us in wherever that is. Dino and I will share a two-bedroom suite. And refuel now rather than later."

"I'll do whatever I can," Faith said, running through her after-landing checklist and shutting down the engines.

As the aircraft's door opened, the air was filled with singing and ukuleles. Stone and Dino walked down the airstairs to be greeted by young women in grass skirts, who festooned them with leis and kisses.

"So far, so good," Dino said.

Stone turned to Faith. "Where are we staying?"

"At the Royal Hawaiian," she said. "It's old but said to be nice. I've ordered a van."

The van pulled up and everyone and their luggage got aboard.

"It's hot," Dino said, fanning himself with his Panama hat.

"It's supposed to be," Stone said.

"Have you ever been to Hawaii?"

"Nope, but I'm told it's hot."

"That was good information," Dino replied.

Stone leaned forward to talk to Faith. "What did you find out about the occupants of the other Gulfstream?"

"They're loaded same as us, two crews and two passengers, plus a dog."

"What kind of dog?"

"Does it matter?"

"Maybe."

"I didn't ask."

"Did you get the names of the passengers?"

"Dickens," she said.

"First names?"

"Charles and Emma. Americans."

"Are we near them in the hotel?"

"I've no idea. That wasn't on your list of requests."

"Do you have any idea what they look like?"

"None at all. It wasn't . . ."

"On my list, I know."

Stone took out a notebook, looked up a number, and dialed it.

"Who are you calling?" Dino asked.

"The FBI tips hotline for Zanian. I want to get this out of the way."

"Do you want them to get to the hotel before we do?"

"Are you kidding? The hotline will take hours to get that to Special Agent Ness. I'm on hold right now."

"Whatever you say."

"I wish everybody said that all the time," Stone said.

The hotel was big and splashy and right on the beach, with Diamond Head in sight.

"That's Diamond Head," Stone said to Dino.

"How do you know? You've never been here."

"I saw it in a movie of the same name, which starred Charlton Heston."

"How old were you at the time?"

"It was on TV."

"I recognized it from *Hawaii Five-O*," Dino said.

They checked in. "By the way," Stone said to the desk clerk, "is there a Mr. Charles Dickens registered here?"

She smiled. "I believe you'll find him in our library," she replied, then went on to the next customer.

"You should have been a detective," Dino said.

They followed a bellman to the top floor of the hotel and were admitted to a spectacular suite.

"Good God!" Stone said. "I didn't ask for the presidential suite!"

"It was all they had," Faith said from behind him. "I just wanted to see it. I'm next door, that way." She pointed. She and her bellman left.

Stone tipped his bellman. "Do you know a guest named Dickens?"

The man shook his head. "No, sir."

"Did you ever get through to anyone on the FBI hotline?" Dino asked.

"No, I left a message."

"I'm sure when they hear the name you left, they'll hang up."

"Good," Stone said.

The bellman threw open the doors to the terrace, and they walked outside. "This is about twenty-five knots of wind," Stone said, leaning into it.

"It must be the altitude," Dino replied, securing his Panama hat before it could blow away.

"We're at sea level," Stone said.

They went back inside and managed to get the doors closed.

"What now?" Dino asked.

"I'm still sleepy," Stone replied.

"Me, too."

They both headed for their respective beds.

Stone was awakened late in the day.

"We're hungry," Faith said on the phone.

"You take the girls to dinner but keep them sober. We may be headed for Midway or Christmas Island next, and I don't want a hungover crew. And if you see any group that looks like another air crew, cozy up to them and find out who they are, what they're flying, who they're flying, and where."

"Gotcha, boss." Faith hung up.

Dino came into his room wearing a hotel robe and looking freshly showered and shaven. "How about some dinner?"

"Call downstairs and book us a table in the main dining room," Stone said, "while I get cleaned up."

Stone went and got cleaned up.

He came into the living room, dressed in a white linen suit.

"Didn't Sydney Greenstreet dress that way in *Casablanca*?" Dino asked.

"Maybe, but not in my size," Stone replied. "Let's go."

They walked into a huge dining room with a band accompanying young women in grass skirts, and with everybody singing "Hawaiian War Chant." They were seated instantly. "Welcome, Mr. Dickens," the maître d' said.

"Is there another party in the dining room named Dickens?"

"No, sir. You'd have to go to our library to find another one." He left menus and a wine list and walked away.

"Did you book the table under Dickens?" Stone asked Dino.

"Maybe. I was still sleepy, and of course, there's the jet lag."

"Swell."

Dino snagged a waiter. "Two mai tais," he said.

"'Mai tais'? Really?"

"It was the only thing Hawaiian I could think of," Dino explained.

Two large pink drinks appeared on the table. Stone took a sip.

"How's your mai tai?" Dino asked.

"Not bad," Stone said. "But it's not Knob Creek."

"I hear they're bringing out one."

"Don't hold your breath." The menu selections all had elaborate descriptions. A waiter appeared.

"I'll have that first thing on the menu," Stone said.

"Me, too," Dino echoed.

Stone ordered a bottle of chardonnay, and the waiter walked away. "Do you have any idea what we ordered?" Stone asked.

"I think it said something about shrimp."

Stone felt somebody's knee nudge him and looked around to find nobody. He looked around again and found two large brown eyes looking up at him expectantly.

"What is it?" Dino asked.

"It's a Labrador retriever," Stone said. "Yellow, just like Bob."

"What does he want?"

Stone suddenly got it. He felt his jacket pocket and found some small lumps. "A cookie," he said, freeing one from the jacket. "Sit," he said. The dog sat, and Stone gave him the treat. He didn't move, except for his tail.

"I beg your pardon," a woman's voice said.

Stone turned to find an attractive woman in a tight, flowered silk dress.

"Is my dog bothering you?"

"He discovered that I have treats in my pocket. I have one at home just like him. What's his name?"

"Felix. And yours?"

"Bob." Stone gave Felix another cookie; it was gratefully

received. "My name is Jack Austen," Stone said. "This is my cousin Fred Austen." He indicated Dino.

"Hello, I'm Frances." They shook hands.

"Would you like to join us for a drink?" Stone asked.

She looked across the dining room. "My party hasn't arrived; I'd love to." She sat down and Felix sat next to her, but not too far from Stone. "What are you drinking?"

"Mai tais," Stone said. "It was the only Hawiian thing Fred could think of."

"Me, too," she said. "Where are you two from?"

"Atlanta," Stone said. "And you?"

"Hartford, Connecticut," she said, after a moment's thought.

"How long have you been in Honolulu?" Dino asked.

"Only a few hours," she said. "We're just passing through."

"What's your final destination?"

"We haven't decided yet."

"'We'? Did you bring along a husband?"

"I don't have one of those. I'm traveling with a friend."

"Did you arrive by air or sea?"

"Air. Private."

"So did we," Dino said. Stone kicked him under the table.

"My friend has a Gulfstream."

Stone shot Dino a glance before he could answer. "Bombardier," Stone said. "It's a Canadian aircraft."

"I'm vaguely familiar," she said.

"Does Felix enjoy air travel?"

"Sort of. He goes to sleep as soon as we're wheels up."

"Bob, too, but we didn't bring him."

"Where did you arrive from?" she asked.

"Manila. We started in Atlanta and flew east to Dubai, then onward."

"So, we're jets that pass in the night," she said. "Do you ever get to Hartford?"

"Only once. Do you get to Atlanta?"

"I think we'll be abroad for some time this trip," she said.

"Next stop?"

"Sydney, I think. Marty hasn't decided yet."

"What business is Marty in?"

"He's an investor."

"So am I," Stone said.

"How'd you make your fortune?" she asked.

"The old-fashioned way. I inherited it."

"So effortless," she said.

"Well, sort of. You have to keep your investment people from stealing from you, and that takes work."

"Like that fellow in New York, recently. I can't remember his name."

"We've been traveling. Don't get a lot of news. Don't care about a lot of news, to tell you the truth."

"Well, never mind, I won't burden you with more."

"Thank you so much. Another mai tai?"

She looked across the room. "My party is arriving," she said, "so I won't have time."

"Another day," Stone said. "In some port or other."

She stood, and they stood with her.

"So nice to see you. Thanks for the drink."

"Same here. Anytime," Stone replied.

"Let's go, Felix," she said, and the dog obediently followed her.

"No leash," Dino said.

"Funny, you were watching Felix, and I was watching her ass. What does that say about us?"

They finished dinner with Key lime pie. "I've had enough Hawaiian music for one evening," Stone said. "Let's have a nightcap at the bar."

"Where's the bar?" Dino asked.

"Across the room, a few steps up. Our path will take us right past Frances's table."

"Lead the way," Dino said.

Stone signed the check and got up just as the band started again, so they had to maneuver through a crowd of dancing tourists.

As the approached Frances's table, Stone took another treat from his pocket. And when they passed, Felix was right at his knee, sitting and pounding his tail on the floor.

"Oops, he caught me," Stone said to Frances. "We've had it with the music."

"Oh, Marty, this is Jack and his cousin, Fred."

Marty stood up and offered his hand. "How do you do?"

"Very well, thank you."

"Jack is a new old friend of Felix's. That is, he has a pocketful of treats."

"I've got one just like Felix at home," Stone said. "We've had it with the music, so we're having a nightcap in the bar. Will you join us?"

"We're still on coffee," Marty said. "Perhaps in a few minutes."

"Don't get lost."

"Don't worry, Felix will deliver us to you," Marty said.

Stone and Dino continued toward the bar, waving at Faith and the crew halfway across the room.

They took a table and ordered Grand Marnier.

"You're right," Stone said. "Marty doesn't seem like Viktor. Maybe he changed his appearance."

Five minutes later, Marty and Frances appeared, led by Felix, who sat in front of Stone. Stone gave him a treat and scratched his ears. He also got a glimpse of a tag attached to Felix's collar.

"This is quite a hotel," Marty said. "I'd like to have seen it before the war."

"Before my time," Stone said.

"Mine, too, but I've seen it in movies. It looks like they must have been having a hell of a good time on the night of Saturday, December 6, 1941."

"Ah, yes," Stone said. "It makes me sad."

"Sad that they were having a good time?"

"Sad that it was the last good time for a lot of them."

"Well, yes, that is sad," Marty replied. "My grandfather was here in Honolulu on the seventh."

"I hope he made it through."

"He made it through until Okinawa, when a kamikaze hit his ship. The ship survived, he didn't."

"My condolences."

"If he'd lived just a couple of months more, I might have gotten to know him," Marty said.

"I guess Okinawa was the last battle of the war," Stone said. "I mean, it was over in May in Europe."

"Yes, the last battle. His last battle."

Stone thought he saw a tear in the corner of the man's eye.

They finished their drinks and said good night. Marty and Frances, at Marty's insistence, stayed behind to pay the bill.

The lights were turned low in their suite when they got back.

"For the honeymooners," Dino said, opening a door to the deck. "Oh, good, the wind has dropped." He stepped outside.

Stone followed him. "Nice moon," he said.

"I'd call Viv," Dino said, "but I've no idea what time it is where she is."

"Where is she?"

"Somewhere in South Asia; I have trouble keeping up, and I left her schedule in New York."

"What did you think of Marty?" Stone asked.

"I liked him. I thought I saw a tear in his eye when he was talking about his grandfather."

"So did I. Do you think Viktor Zanian would ever shed a tear?"

"Nay," Dino replied. "Not about anything."

"Oh, by the way, Felix gave me his phone number."

"I guess the two of you are on intimate terms by now."

"It was on his ID tag, attached to his collar. It's a Connecticut number, 203 area code."

"Well, Frances said she was from Hartford."

"That's right." Stone took out his notebook and jotted down the number. "In case I want to get in touch," he said.

Stone was awakened by a small noise in the middle of the night. He looked at the bedside clock . . . 3:18 AM. He sat up in bed. His gun was in the hotel safe in his closet. He heard the noise again, a *click*, like the door to the suite closing.

Then there was a man in the room, and Stone leapt out of bed and ran for the closet.

"Stone!"

Stone stopped running. "Dino?"

"Who'd you expect?"

"I heard a noise, and my gun is in the hotel safe."

"The noise you heard was the door closing. Somebody was in here."

Stone went to the safe and extracted the .380 pistol. "Okay, lead the way," he said in a low voice.

"What for? They're gone." Dino turned on a living room lamp. "Where's your passport?"

"In the safe," Stone said.

"Your wallet?"

"Everything's in the safe. Yours?"

"Mine is in my bedside drawer. I don't think anybody could have gotten to it without waking me."

"You're thinking Zanian?"

"Who else would care who we are? My wallet is untouched, and your money is in the safe."

"Right," Stone said. "The door to the terrace is still open."

"I heard a door close, so it must have been the front door."

"Must have been," Stone agreed. "I'm going back to sleep."

"Me, too," Dino said. "Good night."

"Good morning," Stone said, leaving the pistol on the bedside table and pulling up the covers.

S tone woke to a ringing noise. The bedside clock read 8:15. He groped for the phone. "Yes?"

"It's Faith. The Gulfstream is departing at ten AM, local," she said. "They're filing for Christmas Island, then Sydney."

"We'd better get dressed then," Stone said. "But we don't want to get there too early and be seen."

"My bunch will go as soon as we're dressed. We'll prep the airplane. You want me to file for Christmas Island?"

"Not yet."

"I'll tune in the clearance frequency on my handheld and monitor it," she said.

Stone hung up and went to wake Dino, but he was already in the shower. "Dino," he yelled, "they're departing at ten AM, local."

Dino turned off the shower and stepped out. "I thought that last night we decided that Marty isn't Zanian."

"Yeah, but I thought of something else: Frances said that they flew in here from the west; that was a lie. Why would she lie to us?"

"Where did they file for?"

"Christmas Island. Why would anyone want to visit there twice?"

"Okay, it's your gas money," Dino said.

They arrived at the FBO at 10:45 and saw the Gulfstream taxiing out for takeoff.

"Drive into the hangar," Stone said to the driver. They were deposited at the foot of the airstairs door, and the waiting crew put their luggage aboard.

"They're rolling," Stone said to Faith.

"Got it. My bet is Midway. You want me to go ahead and file for there? We can always change our destination later."

"Okay."

Faith went forward and cranked up the auxiliary power unit, so they would have air-conditioning, then they closed up and allowed themselves to be towed out of the hangar.

One of the crew came back to where they sat. "Faith says they've already changed their destination to Midway."

"Excellent," Stone said. He turned to Dino. "It's got to be Zanian."

"I still don't think that Marty is Zanian," Dino said.

"You could be right, but I'm betting that Zanian is on that airplane."

"I won't argue that with you."

They took off and headed in a northwesterly direction.

"Tell me again the significance of Midway," Dino said.

"It was always a refueling stop. Juan Trippe, who founded and ran Pan American World Airways, constructed a building there, and his long-range seaplanes, the Pan Am Clippers, stopped for fuel."

"I mean about the war."

"After Pearl Harbor, our U.S. Navy codebreakers cracked the Japanese code. Japan was planning an attack, but they didn't know where. There were references to a place called F, I think, and they thought that was Midway. To find out, they sent a coded message to Midway, telling the operator to send an open message that the island was having trouble with its water condenser. Before long the Japanese broadcast a coded message, which, when broken, said that F was having trouble with its water condensers."

"So they knew it was Midway."

"Right. So they sent a carrier and its escorts to a point northeast of Midway, to lie in wait, figuring the Japanese would attack from the northwest. They were right, and a three-day battle ensured, resulting in the loss of all four Japanese aircraft carriers and a lot of airplanes. It was a turning point in the war. The Japanese never won another battle at sea."

They settled in for a long flight chasing the sun.

Late in the day, approaching Midway, Faith came back. "The Gulf-stream just took off for Manila," she said. "We heard them talking to the center. I've delayed our call to the center until they're out of range. We'll be on the ground about an hour, if you want to stretch your legs, then we'll take off for Manila with a fresh crew."

The old Pan Am building was still on the island, and Stone and Dino took a walk along the beach. The famous gooney birds were still nesting.

They took off. Then Stone and Dino got into pajamas, pulled the shades, and turned in for the night.

Faith woke them in time to shower, shave, and change into fresh clothes. Manila was hot, too.

Faith emerged from the cockpit as they were on their way out of the airplane.

"They're not here," she said.

"What?" Stone asked her, stunned.

"We'll do a ground search at the airport, but as far as I can tell, they didn't land at Manila. The Philippines are a big place, but I'll see what I can find out."

"We've come halfway around the world, and they're not here?" Dino asked.

"They're somewhere," Stone said. "We'll find out where, one way or another. Let's charter a smaller airplane and search the island's airports."

"I checked on that," Faith said. "There are three hundred and fifty-four airports in the Philippine Islands. I was unable to find out how many of them have runways more than five thousand feet long. Where do you want to start?"

Stone was struck silent.

26

Faith came back to the airplane after a trip to the tower. "Okay," she said. "I've talked with both the center and tower crews, and the Gulfstream did land here, refueled and took off again."

"Where did they file for?"

"Midway, but ten minutes after takeoff they changed their destination to Oahu."

Stone was stunned. *"Back to Oahu?"*

"Back to Oahu."

"Well, shit."

"It's clear that they're trying to lose us, and they've gone to great lengths to do so," Faith said.

"Do your people need a night in a hotel?"

"No, I've got a fresh crew who got a solid eight hours on the way from Midway, and by the time they've flown half the route to Oahu, the backup crew will be fresh again. We've no problem for taking off for Oahu as soon as we can refuel and clear out. Customs will be aboard any minute, so hide any weapons you may have."

"All right, that's our plan," Stone said, taking off his jacket and slipping out of his shoulder holster. He took Dino's two pistols and holsters, went aft, and locked them in the airplane's safe, then he went back to his seat and hung up his jacket. Dino was already reading yesterday's *New York Times*. "There's a copy for you on your seat," Dino said.

Customs arrived, checked their passports, and asked the usual questions. The girls all left to stretch their legs.

"This is crazy," Dino said. "You know that."

"I'm satisfied that Zanian is on that airplane, or they wouldn't go to so much trouble to evade us."

"Also," Dino said. "They know that we're not Jack and whatever you named me, or we wouldn't be trying so hard to keep up."

"You have a point," Stone said.

"When we get back to Oahu, I vote we hunt down the son of a bitch and shoot him."

"I don't think the ten-million-dollar reward is for 'dead or alive.'"

"Shit, I forgot about that. All right, let's file our claim for the reward, then shoot him."

"We'll talk about that later, when you're not so angry."

"I think I'm going to be angry for a long time."

Faith returned to the airplane with another customs crew, this one to check them for heading outbound. All this went without incident.

"You're sure you're fresh enough to fly?" Stone asked Faith.

"Our quarters are very comfortable," she said. "We all had showers ashore. Are you ready for takeoff?"

"One question, have we got enough fuel for Oahu, nonstop?"

"Sure. You've got 6,800 miles of range, and Oahu is only 5,300. And the winds are good for us."

"Then let's do it."

The crew went forward, and soon they were taxiing.

One of the crew came back and said to Stone, "Pick up the sat-phone, line one."

Stone picked it up. "Hello?"

"It's Joan. Are you alive or down in the Pacific somewhere?"

"Alive and nearly airborne. We're about to take off from Manila for Oahu."

"That doesn't make any sense at all," Joan said.

"Believe me, I'm aware of that. We're in pursuit, and that's where our quarry is taking us."

"What's Manila like?"

"I've no idea. We never got off the airplane."

"Do you want me to let anybody know?"

"Yes, call Viv Bacchetti and leave a message on her phone if she's not there. Tell her Dino will call her tomorrow."

"Okay, anybody else?"

"Yes, call Brio Ness at the FBI and tell her I said that she can probably pick up what's-his-name at the Royal Hawaiian tomorrow. He's traveling with a man, a woman, and a Labrador retriever."

"I'll tell Bob. He'll be jealous. Anything else?"

"You can reach me on the satphone, if necessary. And tell Brio I'll take a check."

"Okay, happy flying."

"Bye-bye."

As Stone hung up, he was pressed back in his seat from the acceleration. On the way to altitude, he caught a glimpse of the island of Corregidor. He would tell Dino about that to keep him from getting bored.

Stone settled in with yesterday's *New York Times*.

Later, Dino woke from a nap and had a look out the window. "Why don't I see any ships in the Pacific?"

"Because we're flying at fifty thousand feet, and that makes them too small. I don't think you could spot an aircraft carrier. I left a message for Viv from you, saying that you are alive and your feet are dry."

"She'll be comfortable to know that. I hope we're staying at the Royal Hawaiian again," Dino said.

"Why?"

"Because I sent my laundry out there and forgot to get it back."

"That's as good a reason as any to stay there." Stone picked up the phone and pressed the intercom for the cockpit.

"Yes, sir?" a female voice said.

"Tell Faith to make the same arrangements at the Royal Hawaiian as before."

"Yes, sir."

"And tell her to tell the hotel to have Dino's laundry on his bed when we check in."

"Certainly."

Stone hung up. He pulled the cashmere blanket up to his chin and went back to sleep.

27

They landed at Oahu and, after clearing customs, borrowed a golf cart and searched the FBOs for the other Gulfstream. Nothing.

The good news was that, when they checked into the Royal Hawaiian, Dino's laundry was on his bed.

"Feel better?" Stone asked.

"You bet your ass."

"Do you want the music and menu of the main dining room, or something more intimate?"

"I want a steak," Dino said.

They found another restaurant in the hotel and ordered steaks.

When they got back to their suite, there was an envelope slipped under the door. Written on Royal Hawaiian stationery, it read: *I want more cookies.* It was signed, *Felix.* Stone handed it to Dino.

"They're here?" Dino asked.

"Apparently, but under what name?"

"What was the name last time?"

"Marty and Frances, but I can't remember their last names. Can you?"

"Ah, no."

Stone dug out his notebook and looked up a number.

"Who are you calling?" Dino asked.

"Felix."

"Does he have his own phone?"

"He has his own number."

A woman answered. "Yes?"

"I was looking for Felix," Stone said. "Isn't this his number?"

She laughed. "Well, now that you mention it. Felix is indisposed at the moment. He's walking Marty on the beach."

"How long does this operation usually take?"

"Half an hour, but they've already been gone for twenty minutes."

"Poor planning on my part," Stone said. "Perhaps lunch tomorrow?"

"May I bring Felix?"

"I'd be disappointed if you didn't."

"Where and when?"

"In my palatial suite." He gave her the number.

"Will Fred be there?"

"Not if I have anything to say about it, and I will. Noon?"

"Felix and I will look forward to it." She hung up.

"I take it I'm persona non grata at lunch tomorrow," Dino said.

"You're very perceptive."

"She's bringing Felix?"

"Yes."

"You'd better remember to order him something from room service. He's very persistent, as I recall."

"You have a point."

Dino yawned. "I don't know when to get sleepy anymore."

"I think now is a good time," Stone said. "Good night."

The following day, Stone called room service and ordered two lobster salads, a bottle of good chardonnay, lunch for a dog, and a bag of dog treats, all for delivery at, and not before, one PM. "Don't be early," he said to them.

At one minute past noon, Stone's doorbell rang, and he opened it to find Frances and Felix standing there. He let them in, gave Felix a treat, then snaked an arm around her waist and kissed Frances, getting a much warmer reception than he had expected.

"What time is lunch?" she asked, a little breathlessly.

"Not before one o'clock," he said, hanging out the DO NOT DISTURB sign and locking the door. He followed her directly to the bedroom, where she flung back the covers, then undid something and her wraparound dress unwrapped.

Stone was in bed to greet her when she finished. "We couldn't manage this last time," he said.

"I was sorry about that," she replied, taking him in her hand, "but now we can make up for it." She squeezed. "Oh, that was quick."

"No, you were quick. It's just following instructions."

Frances rolled over and pulled him on top of her. "New instructions," she said.

A few minutes before one, Stone unlocked the front door and removed the DO NOT DISTURB sign from the doorknob, then he found them both robes. "Let's not shock the room-service waiter," he said.

"I'll leave that to you," she said. "I'm having lunch right here, and I'm not dressing for the occasion."

The doorbell rang precisely at one o'clock. Stone received the tray on wheels, signed the check, and handed it back. "I'll take it from here," he said to the waiter, replacing the sign and locking the door.

He wheeled the tray into the bedroom. "We won't be disturbed," he said. He served Felix first, then piled up some pillows and handed Frances her lobster salad. "I hope you're not allergic to shellfish," he said, then served himself and poured two glasses of wine and slipped in beside her.

"How long are you here for?" she asked.

"That depends on how long you're here for," Stone replied.

"Only a day or two," she said.

"Then I'll be here a day or two. What is your last name?" Stone asked.

"You pick one, and that's who I'll be," she replied.

"I don't have a preference, as long as I can reach you through Felix. Where will you go from here?"

"To be determined by Marty," she said.

"What is Marty's last name?"

"Whatever you choose for me."

"Is he running from somebody?"

"Why do you ask?"

"Because his routing is odd."

"So is yours. What brought you back here?" she asked.

"I got bored with flying long legs, and when I discovered that it was going to take a week of paperwork to get into Hong Kong, I said, 'The hell with it, let's go back to the States. I've got enough suits.'"

"Why are you interested in Marty?"

"Because where he goes, you go."

"That's very flattering," she said.

"Why don't you just switch Gulfstreams and come with me?"

"First time I've had an offer involving two Gulfstreams."

"Does it appeal to you?"

"It does, but there's a hitch."

"So what? There's always a hitch. They're there to be un-hitched."

"This one is financial. When I met Marty, I let him invest all my money."

"Uh-oh," Stone said. "This is beginning to sound familiar. Has he been in the news lately?"

"Oh, that's right, you never get the news."

"I get the occasional *International New York Times*."

"Is there something in it about Marty today?"

"I haven't read it yet," Stone said. "All I could think about was lunch with you."

"Are you interested in the reward for Marty?"

"How much is the reward?"

"Ten million dollars."

"I don't need another ten million."

She laughed. "Good answer."

"How much are you into Marty for?"

"Two million, plus."

"What are your chances of getting it out of him?"

"I'm not sure. He keeps saying he'll give it to me whenever I want it, but then he dodges."

"Why don't you just tell him to give you your money, or you'll turn him in for the reward?"

Frances sighed. "Because then he'd kill me. I don't know if you've noticed, but we travel with a pair of assassins aboard."

"I had not noticed," he said, wondering how he could have been so stupid. Stone set their clean dishes on the tray, then pushed it out of the room and into the hallway. When he came back, she had kicked off the covers and was spread-eagle on the bed.

Stone put Marty right out of his mind.

S tone woke from a deep sleep to find Frances bending over
him. He kissed her back, then he got out of bed, took her into
the living room and sat her down. "How much time before
Marty is back in the hotel?"

"Maybe a couple of hours, or he could already be back. He can
be unpredictable."

"It's time for you to get out," he said.

"Of here?"

"Of Marty's clutches."

"I agree. Only the promise of my money has kept me with him."

"Can we agree that he's not going to give you your money
back?"

Her shoulders slumped. "Yes. I've been foolish to stick with
him this long."

"Do you understand that, if he thinks you're leaving him, he'll kill you?"

"Yes. More likely, he'll have Mom and Dad do it."

"His parents are traveling with him?"

"No."

"Your parents?"

"Mom and Dad are the assassins," she said. "They're ordinary-looking people, probably in their fifties. They look like half the people in this hotel. They never sit with us. They hover nearby, and they're always armed."

"Whose dog is Felix?"

"Mine, but Marty loves him dearly."

"So, he wouldn't hurt Felix."

"Never."

"Nor order one of his assassins to do it?"

"Never."

"How long would it take you to get your necessities together and to this room?"

She thought about it. "Half an hour."

"What do you need to take with you?"

"My jewelry and a couple of changes of clothes."

"Are you ready to make a move in my direction?"

"Yes."

"Then, for a start, let's stop all the horseshit. My name is Stone Barrington, and I'm a New York attorney. My friend is Dino Bacchetti"—he spelled it for her—"and he's the police commissioner of New York City."

"Is he on duty?"

"No, he just likes to travel. Now, it's your turn."

"Margot, with a—*t*—Chase. I'm a New Yorker. I mostly live on the income from a bequest, now in Viktor's hands."

"Good to have that out of the way."

"What do you want me to do?" she asked.

"Go get the minimum amount of stuff that you need, and bring it back here. Leave Felix with me. If you get back and Marty shows up, drop everything and come back here. Tell him Felix rolled in something dirty, and you're having him groomed, and you have to pick him up. Can you handle that?"

"Yes, I think so."

"About your money: if I get the reward, I'll make you whole from the proceeds."

"What if you don't get the reward?"

"I'll see that you're not left destitute."

"So, I'll have to trust you?"

"It's either that, or trust Zanian."

"I choose you," she said.

"What name is he traveling under?"

"It varies from day to day."

"What name did he use when he checked in here?"

"George Martingale. I'm his wife, Gilda."

"Suite number?"

"Suite 850, on the ocean side."

"All right, I'll wait until you're safely back here before I call it in."

"What's your plan after that?"

"Back to New York. We'll get out of here in the middle of the night and take off as soon as the airport is open; I don't know what time that is, but my pilot can find out."

"All right."

"Where is Zanian's airplane?"

"At Hilo. When he's ready to go, he'll call his crew and have them fly back here to pick us up."

"Next destination?"

"He won't tell me until we're aboard."

"And you won't be aboard," Stone said.

"I'd better go, then. You stay here, Felix. I'll be back, sweetheart." She gave him a treat.

Stone walked her to the door and repeated his cell number twice, making her recite it to him. "If I forget, I'll ring Felix. Answer him."

"Okay, now go, and move fast," he said, closing the door behind her.

As soon as the door closed, Dino emerged from his room. "Don't bother explaining," he said, "I've been listening. You really think you can pull this off?"

"Why not?"

"Well, if she makes it back here alive, then I guess that's half the battle."

"At least half," Stone said.

"You're going to give her two million of the reward?"

"Without her, we couldn't collect the reward," Stone said. "She's got it coming."

"If you say so."

"And you're still getting your five million," Stone said.

"You bet your ass I am. Hey, Felix."

Felix came over and gave him a big kiss.

"Just what I always wanted," Dino said. "Lots of big, wet tongue."

Half an hour later, Stone had briefed Faith. The airport opened for takeoffs at seven AM, and he and Dino were worrying.

"She said half an hour, didn't she?" Dino asked.

"Did you ever know a woman who said 'half an hour' and stuck to it?"

"Are we including my wife?" Dino asked.

"Yes."

"No, I haven't."

"We can't panic because she's not here yet," Stone said.

"When can we panic?"

"Maybe after an hour."

"What do we do when we panic?"

"Call the FBI, tell them about, ah Margot Chase and George Martingale, then get to the airport."

"What then?"

"That depends on what happens," Stone said.

29

The doorbell rang, and Stone opened it. Margot Chase fell into the room, dragging a suitcase on wheels behind her.

"I made it," she said.

"Not in half an hour," Stone replied, "but we'll let that pass."

"There was something important that I couldn't bring," she said.

"What was that?"

"A book where Viktor has recorded the money he's taken and where he's sent it."

"Was it too heavy?"

"I couldn't find it. It's usually in a desk drawer, but he must have taken it with him."

"Never mind that for the moment. Go have your reunion with Felix."

She did so.

Stone dug out Brio Ness's phone number and dialed it. A male voice answered, "Yes?"

"Brio Ness, please?"

"Who's calling?"

"Stone Barrington."

"Does she know you?"

"Ask her."

"Special Agent Ness is not available at the moment."

"What a shame," Stone said. "And she was so looking forward to arresting Viktor Zanian and finding all his money."

"What?"

"Wake her up, if necessary, and tell her to call me immediately, if she wants Zanian's head on a platter. Oh, and I'd hate to be you, if she doesn't get the message *right now*." Stone hung up.

"How long do you think?"

"Half a minute," Stone said, checking his watch. At twenty-eight seconds his phone rang. "Hello," he said.

"This is Special Agent Ness."

"Funny, you don't sound like Special Agent Ness. Convince me."

"Stone," she said, "what the fuck do you want?"

"I want Viktor Zanian's head on a platter. What do you want?"

"Tell me what I need to know."

"I'm in Honolulu and all times will be Hawaiian. You'll have to figure out what time it is where you are."

"All right."

"Viktor Zanian is registered at the Royal Hawaiian in Hono-lulu, under the name of George Martingale. He's in suite 850, on the ocean side. His airplane is parked at Hilo and will pick him up in Oahu, at seven AM tomorrow morning. They will depart shortly after that. Destination: known only to Zanian. He's traveling with a notebook containing an accounting of all the money he's stolen and a list of all the banks where he has hidden it."

"What if we can't make a raid happen that fast and miss him?"

"Then I'm sure you can find a nice, cozy law firm in some darling small town where you can eke out a living defending domestic abuse cases."

"I can't just snap my fingers and produce fifty special agents in Honolulu," she said.

"Then you'd better find somebody who can. Start with your director, and if he can't do it, see if you can get the president on the phone."

She made a furious noise.

"Oh, by the way, Zanian travels with a team of assassins, one each male and female, who are middle-aged, innocuous-looking, and are known by the names of Dad and Mom. You might want to shoot them first and read them their rights later."

"I understand he also has a female companion and a dog."

"I've already detained both of them. I'd haul in the whole outfit, but I don't want to get shot."

"That's selfish of you."

"It is my nature in a conflict to die last, if at all. Will you let me know how this turns out, or will I have to read about it in the Honolulu *Pineapple Picker*?"

She hung up.

"How did she sound?" Dino asked.

"Ungrateful. You do all the work for those people, and they still can't seem to make an arrest."

147

"What's your plan?" Dino asked.

"Funny you should mention that," Stone said. "I have no fucking idea."

"Well, don't you want to be there to witness the whole thing?"

"I'd love to kick in the Gulfstream's door for them, but I didn't bring my bulletproof underwear. How about you?"

"I'd just as soon wait until everybody runs out of ammo," Dino replied.

"Good idea. Now, we should be packed and ready to get out of here before dawn's early light. I'll get Faith working on that now." He picked up the phone.

"Any idea of our destination?" Dino asked.

"Teterboro. Probably without a fuel stop. I intend to sleep in my own bed tomorrow night."

"Alone?"

"To be determined," Stone said.

Margot came over. "Do I get a vote on that?"

"Yes, please. How do you vote on the motion?"

"What's the motion again?"

"Do I sleep in my own bed, alone, tomorrow night."

"I vote no," she said. "And if it somehow passes, I'll veto it."

"I think that answers your question, Dino."

"Did you call Faith?"

"Yes, and I left a message."

After some time, Stone's phone rang. "Yes?"

"It's Special Agent Ness."

"Hi again."

"I've managed to put together a team of twenty-five people by borrowing sheriff's deputies and fruit inspectors."

"Good, what will the fruit inspectors be armed with? Spray guns?"

"We'll loan them shotguns."

"By the way, if you have any intention of impounding Zanian's Gulfstream, you'd better be careful what you shoot at it. It's a twenty-five-million-dollar airplane, new. And who knows, you may even want to fly the thing home."

"How did you know I'll be there?"

"I didn't. Where are you?"

"I just departed San Francisco on a government aircraft."

"'Trust me, you'd enjoy Zanian's Gulfstream more. It has actual windows that you can see out of, and probably has dirty movies available for viewing."

"As jolly as that sounds, I have to put the idea of just getting there and back first."

"As you wish. Can you tell me what time you and your fruit inspectors are going to bust down the hangar doors? We're trying to take off out of here at eight AM, local."

"I can't promise you a time. I'll call you when everything is secure. Don't leave for the airport until then. How many crew and passengers on your airplane?"

"Eight crew and four passengers, one of whom is a Labrador retriever."

"Is that Zanian's dog? If so, I'll have to impound him."

"No relation," Stone said. "He belongs to an acquaintance of mine, so you keep your paws off him."

"All right, I'll take your word for it."

"It's about time you took my word for *something*. By the way, I hope you've got the ten million on you."

"Don't get ahead of yourself," she replied. "We'll have to get you certified, first, before you can even pat me down."

"Sorry, in my enthusiasm I forgot about government red tape."

"Amateurs always make that mistake. Remember, stay where you are, until I give the all clear."

"Just one other thing: there are two Gulfstreams involved here. Mine is the one in the hangar at Signature Aviation. Don't go anywhere near it. Zanian's is in Hilo and probably can't take off before dawn. I suggest you take his airplane on the ground there, then make the crew fly you to Honolulu. That way you can surprise Zanian when he comes aboard, and you can avoid a shootout."

"That's a very good idea. When this is over I'm going to recommend you for a junior special agent's badge, which you can wear on your pajamas."

"My heart is full."

She hung up.

"Okay," Stone said, "everybody relax. We're going to stay here until they've bagged Zanian."

"All three of us?" Dino asked.

"Felix, as well."

30

Early the next morning, Stone got Faith on the phone and
brought her up to date. "We can't fly away until the FBI gives
us the all clear, but I don't see why you and your crew shouldn't
go out there right now, do your preflight inspection and get everything ready to go."

"Okay."

"And you can take our luggage and get it aboard."

"Will do."

"One thing: do not, on any account, let anyone take the airplane out of the hangar. We don't want them to confuse our G-500
with the one flown by the bad guys."

"Got it," she said. "The airplane stays in the hangar."

They hung up.

"I think I'll go for a walk," Dino said. "Felix, you up for that?"

Felix assented.

"Oh, no you don't," Stone said. "We have no idea where Zanian is, and he might spot the two of you and follow you home. We can't have that."

"So, I have to go by myself," Dino said.

"It would be better if you didn't go at all," Stone replied. "That way you can stay out of trouble."

"Sorry about that, Felix," Dino said. "Let's see if we can find a good movie on the TV. You like Lassie?"

"Well," Margot said, stretching and yawning. "I think I'll have a nap."

"Need any help with that?" Stone asked.

"I'll scream, if I get into trouble," she said and headed for the bedroom.

"So, it's you, me, Felix, and Lassie," Dino said to Stone, switching on the TV.

"Pass on the Lassie movie," Stone said. "My apologies, Felix." He thought that, if he tried hard, he might hear Margot screaming for help.

They had exhausted each other twice, when Margot's handbag started ringing. "That can be only one person," she said, "or a wrong number." She got out of bed and shook the phone out of her bag, still ringing. "Hello? . . . Well, of course it's you. Where are you? . . . I'm not there, and I'm not telling you where I am, until I get some answers . . . Well, for a start, what is our next destination? A girl likes to know these things . . . My bags aren't there because

I sent everything to be laundered and dry-cleaned. Everything smelled of tropical sweat."

Stone was regaining consciousness now, and tuning in to her conversation.

"What's our schedule? . . . When are we getting out of here? . . . Felix is at a groomer. He got into something awful, and the smell was unbearable. He should be back soon . . . Now, where are you, and where are we going? . . . What is Lanai? All right, *where* is Lanai? . . . And it has a runway long enough for the Gulfstream? . . . How on earth did you get there? All right, all right, don't tell me anything! Except one thing. I want my money back today. No, no, Viktor, no more delays. I want it wired to my bank at the hour of opening for business, and I'm not budging from Honolulu until that happens . . . Well, then, stick to masturbation. At least you'll be doing it with somebody you love! . . . Okay, it's an old joke, but it has the virtue of being true . . . I'm tiring of being on the airplane with those creeps, Dad and Mom. I have trouble falling asleep with them on the same airplane . . . They are not harmless! She told me they have killed more than two dozen people and never been arrested! . . . Now, I've drawn the line: this is where you come through or where I get off. Take your pick. All right, don't call me again until the money is in my bank and I've spoken to the manager there. You have all the account information. Two and a half million dollars . . . I'm not going to quibble with you over change, just do it!" She hung up.

"Well," Stone said, "*that* was an interesting conversation. I think I can fill in his lines. Did he say anything I couldn't figure out?"

"He says he's going to wire the funds first thing this morning."

"In what time zone?"

"New York."

"Do you think he'll really do it?"

"Possibly. We'll just have to wait and see."

"Are you going to stick to your guns?"

"You're damned right I am. I have a better chance of sharing in the reward than I have getting it back from him."

"The reward will take longer," Stone said.

"Then I'll just have to be patient. I've got enough from my parents' estate to keep body and soul together until they come through. Thank God Viktor never got his hands on that!"

"Good for you." Stone found a tourist map of the islands. "Here's Lanai," he said, pointing to an island south of Oahu. "That's where he is?"

"He said he plans to leave from there."

"So, that's where the airplane is?"

"He didn't say, exactly. For all I know he could be downstairs in the bar."

"That's a big help."

"What I need is a long soak in a hot tub," she said, kicking off the covers.

"Can I watch?"

"You can help," she said. "You can scrub my back."

"I prefer your front."

"That, too."

"You go get started," Stone said. "I'll be along shortly."

She left the room, and he heard the tub running. Stone called Brio Ness and got the same annoying young man he'd spoken to last time. "Call her on the airplane and tell her to call me," he said.

"And who is this, again?"

"It's Stone Barrington, and you can tell her I have an update on what's happening here." He hung up. Ten minutes later his phone rang. "Yes?"

"It's Ness. Do you know how hard it is to get to sleep on an airplane?"

"Yes, and it's not particularly hard, if you have a clear conscience."

"And why wouldn't I have a clear conscience?"

"I'm not absolutely certain you have a conscience at all," he said. "Do you want more info?"

"Yes!"

"There's another Hawaiian airport in play."

"'In play'?"

"He may not be in Honolulu, and his Gulfstream may be on its way to Lanai."

"Isn't that a Hawaiian front porch?"

"No, it's an island off Maui that's owned mostly by a tech wizard, and it has a runway long enough for the Gulfstream."

"Are you sure it's there?"

"No, but Zanian just called somebody and hinted that he was, and that he might be leaving from there."

"Leaving for where?"

"No idea."

"So, let me get this straight; I've got people at Hilo and Honolulu and both he and the airplane might be on Lanai?"

"Possibly."

"I don't want to hear about possibly! I want certainty!"

"Do you know anybody at any government agency who can

produce a live satellite shot of the airport at Lanai and who can identify a Gulfstream 500 on sight? Who can read the tail number?"

"Probably."

"Then you'd better get ahold of him right now and put him to work! Where are you now? What's your ETA to Honolulu, or somewhere?"

"I'll see what I can do," she said, ignoring his question, then hung up.

Stone, muttering to himself, went looking for a bath.

An hour later, leaving Margot in a pristinely clean state, he heard his phone ringing in the bedroom and went there to answer it. "Hello?"

"It's Faith," his pilot said. "Your airplane is gone."

S tone's knees went a little weak. "What do you mean, my airplane is gone?"

"Gone, as in not there."

"Not in the hangar? Maybe they towed it out to wash it, or something."

"It's not on the ramp, and the FBO isn't even open, yet."

"Check with the tower."

"I have already done so, after half a dozen attempts to get them to answer. They just opened."

"And?"

"And zip. They have no information on the whereabouts of your airplane."

"I'll be out there as soon as I can," Stone said.

"Please."

Stone hung up.

"What's wrong?" Dino asked. "You've turned an odd shade of white."

"The airplane is gone."

"Zanian's airplane?"

"No, *my* airplane."

"You mean like, *poof*, it's gone?"

"Like *poof*," Stone said, looking for underwear and socks. Faith had taken all his things to the airport, except for one change of clothes. He got his pants on.

"Come on, Stone," Dino said. "There must be some logical reason for this. Airplanes don't just go *poof*."

"*Poof* is what we've got on our hands. I'd planned to fly that aircraft across a chunk of the Pacific and home today, but I've got to find it first."

Dino got dressed, too. "Well, let's go, I'm as interested in this as you are."

"Not quite," Stone said, heading for the door. Felix met him there. "Did Faith take Felix's bag with all his food and toys?"

"Faith took everything."

They got into a cab. Stone gave the address to the driver and then sat, dumb.

"I hope you're thinking about this problem," Dino said after a while.

"How could I think about anything else?"

"Good point."

They screeched to a halt in front of the FBO, where the lights were just coming on. Stone found a lone young woman busying herself with opening.

"I'd like to report a missing airplane," Stone said to her.

"That happens sometimes. There are thieves everywhere. Is it a single-engine or a twin?"

"It's a Gulfstream 500 jet."

The young woman froze. "What are you talking about?"

"Do you remember having the linemen put it in your hangar?"

"Yes."

"Well, it's not in your hangar now. Do you see it on the ramp?"

She opened a door, stepped outside, then returned after a couple of minutes. "You're right," she said.

"Thank you."

"Should I call the police?"

"Well, if the airplane isn't in your hangar and it's not on the ramp, then it must be in the air," Stone said.

"Right."

"What do you suppose the police could do about that?"

"Find it when it lands?"

"Lands where?"

"You're right again," she said. "So, I should do nothing?"

"For the moment," Stone said. He got a cup of water from the watercooler and downed it. His phone rang.

"Hello?"

"It's Ness."

"Where are you?"

"In your airplane."

"Oh? I didn't know you were type-rated for a G-500."

"I'm not, but we brought a G-500 crew with us to fly Zanian's airplane back. They weren't doing anything so, I thought, what the hell?"

"You've *stolen* my airplane? Who do I call about that, the FBI?"

"You used to be a cop, didn't you?"

"I did."

"Wasn't there ever a time, when you were in pursuit of a perp, when you took a civilian's car for the chase? Happens in the movies all the time."

"It happened to me twice in fourteen years, but I never commandeered anybody's airplane."

"'Commandeered'? I like that word. Has an official ring to it."

All Stone could do was sputter. "Where are you going?" he asked.

"Don't worry, the tanks are all full. We checked."

"Where?"

"We're headed to Hilo first. If he's not here, we'll try Lanai. By the way, this is a *really* nice airplane. Did you come by it honestly? Usually, when people have personal assets this expensive, they've acquired them by, shall we say, *extralegal* means?"

"I paid cash," Stone said. "After-tax cash."

"Well, I guess that means we don't get to keep it, doesn't it?"

"Don't worry, you can keep Zanian's airplane when you arrest it."

"Oh, good. Gotta run." She hung up

Dino and Faith walked into the FBO. "It's nowhere to be found," he said.

"I just got a call from Brio Ness," Stone said. "The FBI has commandeered the airplane to search for Zanian."

"Can they do that?"

"Do you remember the time when you and I were chasing an armed robber, and we threw an old lady out of her station wagon and took it?"

Dino smiled. "Yeah, I remember. She raised hell about that with the captain, didn't she? Good thing we caught the son of a bitch."

"Well, I'm going to raise hell with the director of the FBI about it," Stone said.

"If she catches Zanian, it won't do any good."

"Then I'll use this to press for early delivery on the reward."

"Do we still get the reward if we're not there when she captures him?"

"Damn right, we do."

A while later, Faith walked over. "Stone, your airplane just landed and is taxiing in," she said.

Stone looked out the window and discovered that it had begun to rain, hard. The G-500 turned off the runway and disappeared into the gloom.

"Special Agent Ness seems to be headed for the main terminal," Faith said.

"She would," Stone replied, "knowing that I'm waiting at the FBO."

S tone's cell phone rang. "Yes?" he said, wearily.

"It's Margot."

"Well, hi there. You awake?"

"Yes. Are you at the airport?"

"Yes, and all your luggage is here. Unfortunately, the FBI has, sort of, borrowed my airplane to look for Zanian."

"Well, he should be easy to find now."

"Why is that?"

"Because he just called me and asked if I was coming with him."

"And what did you tell him?"

"I asked him if he had transferred my two and a half million to my account. I called the bank manager, and he wasn't in yet, so I left a message."

"Did you tell Zanian that?"

"Yes. I told him I'd get back to him as soon as the bank opens."

"And how did he take that?"

"He said they were refueling, and he would wait until he had full tanks."

"Did he say where he was refueling?"

"Yes, at the airport."

"Which airport?"

"I just assumed he was at the Honolulu airport, if he's waiting for me."

Stone thought about that. "I'll call you back." He hung up and turned to Faith. "What sort of paint job does Zanian's airplane have?"

"I've never seen it until now, but most G-500s seem to have the standard Gulfstream paint design. If somebody wants a corporate logo or something, they have it done in a graphics shop and glued on over the original paint."

Stone called the satphone on his airplane and a man answered. "Yes?"

"Special Agent Ness, please. Do you know how to connect me to the cockpit?"

"Sure. Hang on."

"Special Agent Ness," she said.

"Did you just land at Honolulu?" he asked.

"We were going to, but the weather turned foul, and we couldn't get down. We're in a holding pattern."

Stone looked out the window; it was still raining heavily. "Zanian landed at Honolulu fifteen minutes ago."

"How do you know that?"

"Because I'm at the airport, and I saw him land. I thought it was you, in my airplane. The paint jobs are similar."

"Holy shit! Keep him there until the weather clears. The forecast said it would be less than an hour."

"How am I supposed to do that? Handcuff the airplane to the fuel truck? You should have your office call the tower and ground him."

"I don't know if we have the authority."

"The tower is federal. You're federal. What's the problem?"

"Okay, I'll get started on the red tape."

"Just get your director out of bed and have him make the call. That should impress an air traffic controller. Even better, have him call the head of the FAA!"

"Sit tight," she said.

Stone hung up and looked at the anemometer over the FBO's counter: it was gusting forty knots.

"What did Ness say?" Dino asked.

"She said to sit tight."

"That's helpful."

"Yeah, the FBI is always so very helpful."

"Didn't you read the tail number on that airplane when it landed?"

"In this visibility?"

"How did he land in this visibility?"

"Auto-land," Stone said. "It will fly the airplane right down to the runway and to a full stop."

"Then why doesn't Ness's pilot use that to land your airplane?"

"The original owner didn't want to pay for auto-land. I've ordered the equipment, but it will be months before it can be built and installed."

164

"Next time, spend the money."

"I have spent the money, I just haven't got the goods yet."

"This is very annoying," Dino said.

"I'm so sorry to have inconvenienced you," Stone said, dead-pan. "You know, it would be very helpful if you would run over to the main terminal and shoot out the nosewheel tire on Zanian's airplane."

"Why didn't I think of that? Oh, because it's underwater, out there, and I couldn't stand up in the wind."

"You always have an excuse, don't you?"

"When I do, it's a good one. Tell you what, I'll loan you my gun, and you can do it."

"It's underwater out there, and I couldn't stand up in the wind," Stone replied.

"Now who has excuses?"

Faith spoke up, "Maybe I could ask the terminal manager to leave the fuel truck parked in front of the airplane, so it can't taxi."

"Now, *that* is good thinking," Stone said. "Do you think he'll do it?"

"Well, I had a very pleasant conversation with him after we landed. He asked me to dinner, but I think he's married."

"Why do you care? You're not going to have dinner with him, are you?"

"No, but he might get insistent."

"Tell him the FBI is on the way to arrest somebody on the airplane."

"He'll ask me how I know that. What do I do then?"

"Lie to him."

"What lie would I use?"

"Tell him you'll come over there when it stops raining and do something very nice to him."

Faith turned bright pink. "I am *not* going to do that."

"Of course not. You're just going to *tell* him you will."

"Certainly not! You can fire me, if you like, but I won't do that, and I won't tell him that I will!"

"If I fired you, how would I get home?"

"Good point," she said. "Let's drop the matter."

"I apologize, Faith," Stone said sheepishly.

"Let's not talk about it anymore," she said, picking up a magazine and pretending to read it.

Stone's phone rang. "Yes?"

"It's Margot."

"What's happening?"

"The bank manager called. The funds have been deposited."

"Congratulations! You're probably the only one of his victims to get a refund!"

"What should I do?"

"Call him and tell him the money has arrived, and you'll go with him, but right now, the cabs aren't running because of the storm. And find out how long that will delay his takeoff. Also, see if you can wheedle out of him where he's going."

"I'll do what I can," she said, and hung up.

33

S tone looked out the window. "Is it my imagination, or is the weather letting up?"

"It's not your imagination," Dino said. "I can see the outline of the terminal across the way."

"I think I can see the fuel truck," Stone said, straining to see.

"I'm here," a voice said.

Stone turned and looked. "Hello, Margot." Felix trotted over and nudged him for a cookie. "Hi, Felix," Stone said, supplying the treat.

"Where's my luggage?"

"In that pile over there," he said, pointing.

"Not aboard the airplane?"

"We don't have an airplane yet."

"Stone," Dino said. "Look across the way."

Stone looked out across the runway and could clearly see the terminal building and the fuel truck on the ramp. What he could not see clearly was a G-500. Then a faint rumble turned into a roar and the G-500 came tearing down the runway and lifted off. He turned and looked at the radar display behind the counter. They were on the rear edge of a big area of yellow and red precipitation. "Shit!" he cried. "He must have taxied when the weather started to lift. He was just sitting there, at the end of the runway, waiting for takeoff visibility!"

"That seems like a logically accurate assumption," Dino observed, "especially the part about taking off, since we just saw it happen."

Stone called the satphone on his airplane, and it rang and rang but was not answered. Then, as he watched, his Gulfstream set gently down on the runway and turned off toward the FBO.

"And that would appear to be your airplane," Dino said.

They watched as it taxied toward them on the ramp, then turned 180 degrees. Linemen went out and chocked the wheels, and the airstairs door opened.

"Look who's here," Stone said, as Brio Ness emerged, briefcase in hand.

"Get it refueled," Stone said to Faith. "And lock the doors so Ness and her people can't get back aboard. And get your people out there and start your preflight."

Special Agent Ness entered the FBO and looked around. "Is there such a thing as a drink around here?" she asked nobody in particular.

"At nine in the morning?" Stone asked. "The watercooler is over there."

She went and drank two cups of water, then looked out the

window toward the main terminal. A sunbeam illuminated it. "Where's Zanian's airplane?" she demanded.

"It took off about ten minutes ago," Stone said. "It was quite a sight. I'm sorry you missed it."

"How could he do that?"

"He simply waited for the weather to lift, then did it."

"Where's he bound for?"

Stone turned to Margot. "Any info on that?" he asked.

"Viktor said he was going to Acapulco."

"Yeah," Dino cut in, "that's what he said before he flew to Honolulu."

Ness had collapsed into a chair and was shouting into her cell phone. She hung up and looked at Stone. "I want a lift to Acapulco," she said.

"Not until I have it in writing from you that I am entitled to the ten-million-dollar reward," he said.

"But I haven't captured him."

"Not my fault," Stone said. "I told you, correctly, where to find him, but you didn't act quickly enough."

"We couldn't land in that weather! My pilot said you don't have auto-land."

"I don't believe there is a weather limitation on the reward," Stone said. "Let's have it, and on the Bureau's letterhead."

"I'll commandeer your airplane again!"

"Sure. Show me the court order."

She looked at her watch. "The courts won't open . . ."

"I'll settle for the letter from you confirming that I get the reward."

"No."

"The papers will love this," Stone said. "I can see the headline: FBI SPECIAL AGENT NESS (NO RELATION) FUCKS UP ZANIAN ARREST IN HAWAII!!!"

"No, no, no!"

"Or you can give me the letter, and I'll fly you to Acapulco."

She opened her briefcase, fished out a sheet of stationery and began to write.

"There's a computer over there on the counter. Write it there and use their printer," Stone said.

"You're welcome to my computer," the manager said, "and our printer is color. Is Microsoft Word okay?"

"Okay," Ness said. She walked across the room, sat down at the desk, and began to type, while Stone looked over her shoulder and made suggestions about the wording. She used the print button.

"There you go," Ness said.

"Just sign it," Stone said, offering his pen. "And with your own name, not Amelia Earhart's."

She signed it and handed it to him. Stone read it again, folded it neatly, and handed it to Dino. "Witness that," he said, "then guard it with your dear life."

"Nah, I'm a party to it." He got the FBO manager to witness it, then put it into his inside jacket pocket. "The letter is now witnessed and in the custody of the NYPD."

"How much longer to refuel?" Stone asked Faith.

"Twenty minutes, or so. They didn't use all that much."

"File for Acapulco," he said, "then unlock the doors."

She sent someone out with the key, then got on the phone.

"Okay," Stone said to the rest of the crew. "Get the luggage aboard, including Special Agent Ness's, and prepare the cabin for takeoff." They sprang into action, more or less.

"Can I take my SWAT team?" Ness asked.

"Order one up in Acapulco," Stone said. "They speak the language."

Half an hour later, they were taxiing.

They had been in the air for twenty minutes when Faith called on the intercom. "They've changed their destination to Oakland."

"Change our destination to our final," Stone said, then hung up.

Ness looked worried. "What is your final destination?" she asked.

"Well, since they're not going to Acapulco, there's no point in landing there, is there? Change your SWAT team to Oakland."

"What if they change it again?"

"Then you can change your SWAT team again. Meantime, our final destination is Teterboro, New Jersey."

"New York?"

"After a bit of a drive."

"Oh, what the hell," she said.

34

A couple hundred miles west of Oakland, Ness completed her phone calls and instructions to her SWAT team and made sure they had a copy of the warrant for Zanian.

She sat back in her reclining chair. "Could I have a large Scotch on the rocks, please?" she said to the flight attendant.

"Would you prefer a blend or a single malt?" the woman asked. "We have Laphroaig and a Talisker," she said.

"The Talisker," Ness replied, and it was quickly in her hand. "Stone?"

"Yes, Special Agent?"

"You can call me Brio."

"Yes, Brio?"

"I don't have a bed in New York. Can you provide me with one?"

"Of course, and with dinner, too."

"Who else will be there?"

"Just you," he said. "Margot has chosen to go home to her apartment."

"Thank you, I accept."

Stone picked up the satphone and made the arrangements.

"How long till Teterboro?"

"Seven hours. We've got a tailwind."

"I'm sleepy," she said, setting down her empty glass, which was whisked away by the attendant.

"I'm not surprised. Sleep."

She sank into her seat, and Stone draped a light cashmere throw over her inert body.

Dino looked over at her. "First time I've ever seen an FBI special agent do that. I didn't know they slept."

"They do after a long day's work and a double Scotch," Stone said.

Dino waved at the flight attendant and ordered. "I think I'll try that," he said, taking a gulp of the Scotch.

Stone spread a throw over him, and took his glass away as his fingers relaxed. He ordered a Knob Creek for himself as the satphone rang beside him. "Yes?"

"It's Joan. Are you still on the planet?"

"I am, and we're approaching the coast of California. Tell Fred we'll be landing in about seven hours and to meet us."

"Who's 'us'?"

"Special Agent Ness. Let Helene know we'll need dinner, no matter what time we arrive."

"Should I have the maid ready a room for your guest?"

"That remains to be negotiated."

"We'll be ready for everything."

"By the way, I have a letter, in Dino's possession, stating that I'm to be paid the ten-million-dollar reward."

"Is it genuine?"

"It is, signed by Special Agent Ness and witnessed by a Hawaiian. I shall want you to present it to the director of the FBI for payment."

"In person?"

"A copy, via FedEx, please. You retain the original, in case there's an argument."

"So, you caught Zanian?"

"No, but I made it possible for the FBI to. Not my fault that they blew it."

"Are they going to see it that way?"

"To be announced."

"I shouldn't hold my breath, then?"

"Not for very long."

"Okay, boss, I'll get on it. Oh, I almost forgot: Lance Cabot called and wondered if you would be interested in the whereabouts of Mr. Zanian."

"Can you patch me through to him?"

"I can try. If I push the wrong button, call him direct."

"Right."

There was a squawk, and then the smooth voice of the director of the Central Intelligence Agency filled the satphone. "Stone, where are you?"

"About a hundred miles west of California. Please note that, for once, it does not appear to be on fire."

"What a nice change. Did Joan give you my message?"

"She did, piquing my curiosity."

"Have you found Zanian?"

"No, but I saw his G-500 take off from Honolulu this morning."

"Was he inside it?"

"One can only suspect. Can you confirm that?"

"No, but I suspect it to be so, too."

"Do you have any inspiration regarding his destination?"

"It ain't Acapulco," Lance said.

"I didn't think it would be. Any further thoughts?"

"I hear Santa Barbara, in an hour or so. He has a house there."

"That's the best guess I've heard all day. Is it worth having a SWAT team there to meet him?"

"It couldn't hurt, but the man is elusive by nature, so don't make any promises you can't keep."

"Always good advice," Stone replied.

"Do you expect to collect the price on his head?"

"I have a letter to that effect from the agent in charge of the case."

"Well, that's better than a note on a paper bag."

"Considerably better, I hope."

"You can hope. Call me when you're back home and let me know how things went. If the director turns out to be recalcitrant, let me know. I may be able to help. Goodbye, Stone."

"Goodbye, Lance." He hung up. "Now, why didn't I call him sooner?" he said aloud to himself.

"Call who?" Brio asked sleepily.

"Santa H. Claus."

"Oh."

"I am reliably informed by someone who is reliably informed, that Zanian is headed for Santa Barbara. I'm also told he has a house there."

"Then let's land at Santa Barbara," she said.

"Thank you, but I'm through chasing my tail. If you want to have a SWAT team there, good luck to you. You might order up a search warrant for his house, too."

Ness picked up the satphone and went to work.

35

Once back at his house in New York, Stone sent Fred up with his bags and Brio up with hers. She could choose her own room. Then he settled in at his desk and waited for Joan to show up. It didn't take her long.

"You look oddly well-rested."

"I didn't suffer from lack of sleep."

"Who's upstairs?" she asked.

"Brio Ness. I don't know in what room."

"I'll find out."

"No need to disturb her."

"Any instructions?" she asked.

"Just get that letter to the director of the FBI."

"It's already there. I found a courier service."

"Heard anything?"

"Nope."

"Get me Lance Cabot, please."

She buzzed Stone a moment later. "Lance on one."

"I'm home," Stone said.

"In the company of Mr. Zanian, I hope."

"Sadly no. I've been thinking about the Middle East."

"Lots of people do."

"Is there some small country there, without a treaty, that might shelter Zanian?"

"Undoubtedly," Lance said. "If Mr. Zanian has enough cash to impress a top diplomat or, perhaps, a sultan."

"Do you have one in mind?" Stone asked.

"That depends on whether Mr. Zanian had the foresight to become a Muslim."

"I hadn't considered that."

"It's worth considering."

"Which country?"

"The Sultanate of Saud," Lance said. "The Sauds are cousins of the Saudis, but not as rich."

"Who is?"

"Hardly anyone."

"How much would it take to impress the sultan?"

"Well, Mr. Zanian deposited one hundred forty million dollars in the World Traders Bank today, in the Caymans."

"Wow! Did he steal that much?"

"Estimates are north of two billion. I think his net worth would impress the sultan to the extent of offering him shelter, quietly, in his country."

"How do we find out?"

"I suppose you'd have to know someone who knows the sultan."

"Does anyone I know, know the sultan?"

"Perhaps."

"The only person I can think of who might know the sultan would be you."

"The sultan and I have had dealings in the past."

"Is your arm long enough to poke an elbow in the sultan's ribs?"

"Perhaps."

"In that case, is there something I can do for you?"

"There might be," Lance replied.

"Don't be coy, Lance. What do you want?"

"Dame Felicity Devonshire," Lance said, referring to the head of MI6, the British foreign intelligence service, "is not speaking to me—that is, she is not returning my calls. Find out why, and I will give you entrée to the Sultan of Saud."

"Plain enough," Stone said. "I'll see what I can do." He hung up and looked for Dame Felicity's private number. The two of them were longtime friends and occasional lovers, her country house on the Beaulieu River in England being the neighbor of his place. He dialed the number, and to his surprise, she answered.

"I wondered when you'd get around to calling," she said reprovingly.

"I've been lost in the Pacific for the past week," Stone said.

"My recollection is that telephone service extends to that region of the planet, as it does to all regions. Apparently, Lance Cabot was able to reach you there."

"Actually, I'm home again in New York, and I reached him. He is distraught."

"Oh, really? Whyever would that be?"

"He fears that he has accidentally offended you in some way."

"'Accidentally,' did you say?"

"Yes. Lance would never intentionally offend you, Felicity. He's too fond of you for that."

She emitted a short snort. "I doubt it." But she sounded as if she might be softening.

"I'm absolutely certain of his affection for you, Felicity. Why are you torturing the poor fellow?"

"Well, I'm glad he's noticed," she said.

"Believe me, he has noticed and he is, as I have said, distraught. Don't you think you could give him a call and put him out of his misery?"

"I know an assassin or two who could do that with ease."

"I was speaking metaphorically," Stone said, "as you well know."

"Well, I will be at this number for a half hour or so, if he would like to ring me."

"I'm certain he would. How are you?"

"I'm quite well, thank you. When are you coming over?"

"I'm embroiled in something right now. But when I get it sorted out, I would love to pay you a visit."

"I'll hold you to that, Stone," she said, then hung up.

Stone called Lance. "I've spoken to Felicity," he said. "And while she has not divulged the source of her hurt, she has deigned to accept your call at the private number during the next half hour."

"Oh, she has deigned, has she?"

"That was my interpretation, not hers. You'd better get your ass in gear, pal, or you're going to screw up again."

"Oh, all right."

"And right after that, you can give your friend, the sultan, a call and see if he's harboring a criminal I know."

But Lance had already hung up.

Joan buzzed. "Special Agent Ness is ensconced in the guest room next to the master suite," she said. "And I have informed her that you'll be having a late dinner in your study and that dress is casual, as you like to say. I take it that's code for nude."

"Let's call it dressing down," Stone said. "Thank you." He hung up. He thought of calling Lance but decided he'd better wait to hear from him.

Lance called back to confirm that Zanian would be staying with the Sultan of Saud. Stone wondered how easy it was to get a sultan on the phone, but Lance always found a way.

Stone was still finding his way through Earth's time zones, but he thought it best if he operated on the information contained in his wristwatch, which he had been resetting periodically. He went upstairs, unpacked his clothes, and filled the laundry hamper with what had to be laundered, then he got into a shower.

He had gotten out and was drying himself when someone called.

"Yoo-hoo."

Stone wrapped a smaller towel around himself and walked into his bedroom; Brio was sitting on the end of his bed. "'Yoo-hoo'? In what decade of this century are we operating?"

"The present day. Anyway, it had the desired result, which was to bring you out of hiding."

"I suppose it did, if you consider the shower hiding." He sat down beside her on the bed.

"That's far enough," she said. "More than that, it's close enough."

Stone reached behind him and pointed a finger between his shoulder blades. "I have an itch where I can't quite reach it. Could you help, please?"

She looked at his back, then scratched the correct spot for him.

"Thank you," he said. Her touch was not unaffectionate. "That is a feeling of relief."

"I had a hint that you were seeking relief of some sort," she said, drily.

"What else is on offer?" he asked.

"I had hoped to be offered a drink," she said.

"If you can wait a couple of minutes while I dry my hair and dress, I will take you by the hand and lead you to the watering hole." He got up and walked to the bathroom door, then stopped and looked over his shoulder. "You can watch, if that would please you."

"Oh, please!"

"Another cliché from another era. You're full of them!"

"You're full of something, too," she said, "but it's not clichés."

Stone blew his hair dry and brushed it, then went into his dressing room and got into underwear, trousers, shirt, shoes, socks, and a tweed jacket. He walked back into the bedroom. "The sun is officially over the yardarm, somewhere, so come with me."

They walked down the stairs, which gave Ness an opportunity to view the pictures hung there.

"Very nice paintings," Brio said. "Who chooses them for you?"

"Oh, please!" he said. "To coin a cliché. I am the son of a painter of great accomplishment. I learned about art at her knee, from watching her create it."

They walked on toward the study. "You seem to have a number of canvases signed by a Matilda Stone. Any relation?"

"I had the good fortune to be her son."

"You're right. She's a painter of great accomplishment."

"My mother thanks you." They walked into the study, where Fred had already lit a fire. "You said you were dying for a drink, I believe? What will you have?"

She pointed at a bottle of Talisker. "That," she replied, "if you please."

"Over ice?"

"Please."

He poured it and then a Knob Creek for himself. He put both drinks on a small, silver tray and took it to the sofa, where she had settled herself.

"You have a nice mix of period pieces and the more recent," she said.

"I inherited the house and its contents from my great-aunt. I sold off some of her pieces for cash to do a complete remodel and kept the others in storage, along with the china and silverware and some pictures. The rest I have added over time."

"That little tray on which you served our drinks is a lovely thing," she said.

"It was made by a Boston silversmith named Revere," he replied.

"Not *that* Revere," she said.

"*That* Revere. My great-aunt had a complete tea service and some table serving pieces of his, too."

"Well, if you're ever broke, those would bring a pretty price."

"I've been broke, and I didn't like it," Stone said, "but I managed to hold on to the silver. May I get you another drink?"

"Let's give the first one a little more time to do its work," she said.

"No rush. I've been meaning to tell you that I'm pursuing a lead on Mr. Zanian."

"Oh, don't call him 'Mister,'" she said. "He doesn't deserve the respect."

They dined on a thick slab of country pâté, then thinly sliced veal, then blueberry pie for dessert. They moved to the sofa for cognac.

"That was delicious," Brio said.

"You look delicious," Stone replied, kissing her behind the ear. "Shall we find out?"

"I don't suppose I can persuade you to wait a little longer," she said.

"That's very perceptive of you."

"Here, on the sofa, or shall we make a move?"

"Let's make a move," Stone replied, and they did.

She disappeared into the guest dressing room while Stone simply stripped off and got into bed. When she came out, she was wearing the guest terry-cloth robe.

"May we have the lights off?" she asked.

"If you prefer. I was looking forward to looking at you."

She flicked off the bedside lamp, shucked off the robe, and got into bed with him.

"I'm sure this is improper," she said.

"I hope so. It's more fun that way."

Then she seemed, finally, to make a decision and turned into his arms. Things moved more quickly after that, and they were soon enjoined, with her on top.

"You enjoy being on top, don't you?"

"What?"

"Not just in bed, in general."

"This seems to be working rather well," she breathed. "Would you prefer something else?"

He rolled them over, emerging on top. "I'd prefer this, for the moment. Then we can explore, if you like." As he began there was a terrible buzzing noise. "What is that?" he asked.

"It's my cell phone, and that particular noise means it can't go unanswered under any circumstances."

He rolled off her. She ran for her bag and picked up the phone. "Special Agent Ness," she said, then stepped into the dressing room and closed the door behind her. By the time she returned, Stone had cooled down markedly.

"Sorry about that," she said.

"Was it really that important?"

"That was a Zanian alert," she said. "His airplane just took off from Santa Maria, in the Azores."

"Refueling stop," Stone said. "Do they know his destination?"

"No, not yet."

"Perhaps I can help."

"How could you possibly do that?"

"By telling you, possibly, his destination."

"All right, what's your best guess?"

"The Sultanate of Saud," Stone said. "And it's not a guess. It's an informed judgment."

"Why not Saudi Arabia? We've no extradition treaty with them."

"Zanian unwisely took a large investment from an important prince and failed to return it when he fled."

"How could you know that?"

"That's not important, but my source says it's true, and that's good enough for me."

"Then your source must be in the Saudi government."

"It is not."

"Then it must be in the highest echelon of American intelligence."

Stone opened the bedside drawer, fished out a card, and handed to her.

She looked at it. "Associate director and adviser to the director? Don't be ridiculous! Do they print those down at your cigar stand?"

"I don't indulge in cigars, and the card is genuine, as is the information upon it."

"Good God! You've been spying for the Agency all this time?"

"I'm not a spy, and you had only to ask, if you wanted to know what my connections were."

"Well, I had heard that you are a close, personal friend of the president," she said, "whatever that means."

"It means that we are close, personal friends," Stone said. "It would be a mistake to read anything else into it."

"Good God!"

"I think you would be less anxious if you could simply believe that anything I tell you is true, instead of a lie."

"Can you prove your connection to the president?"

"Yes, but I decline to do so. You are a high official of our nation's most important investigative agency, and that you didn't know these things means that you are either negligent or uninterested or both. Surely you have read my file."

"What makes you think you're important enough to even have a file with us?"

"You'll know that after you've read my file."

"Excuse me," she said. She got up, left the room, and soon, Stone could hear the clicks of a laptop keyboard. After a few minutes of this, he drifted off to sleep.

He woke after sunup and realized that he was alone in bed. He got up and went to the guest bedroom next door and found the bed made and her luggage gone. The bell sounded that meant breakfast was on the way up in the dumbwaiter. He went back to his suite, took the tray and set it on the bed, then adjusted the bed's angle, got into it and began to eat.

S tone was at his desk the next morning when Joan buzzed. "Special Agent Ness on one."

Stone picked up. "Stone Barrington."

"Good morning."

"If you say so."

"I'm sorry I vanished last night, but you were sound asleep, and I didn't want to wake you."

"Thank you. I was grateful for the sleep. Anything else?"

"I would like to come and see you this morning and bring a friend."

Stone couldn't help laughing. "A threesome? At this time of day?"

"Of course not! And mind what you say on this line."

"Are we being recorded?"

"Not to my knowledge."

"If you're not sure, then you should choose your words more carefully."

"It's a male friend," she said.

"There you go again."

"Will you stop misinterpreting me?"

"If you will think and speak more clearly. Let's start over: What do you want?"

"I want to bring a colleague to your office for a meeting."

"There, that's better. Who is your colleague?"

"A person whose presence will allow me to make decisions quickly."

"All right. When would you like to come?"

"Now."

"Right this minute?"

"We are sitting in a car outside your office."

Stone laughed again. "Ring the bell under the brass plate at the door," he said. He buzzed Joan. "Ms. Ness and a colleague are about to ring the front bell. Please show them into my office." He hung up and walked over to the seating area and waited. A moment later, Joan showed in Brio Ness and a man Stone had met once before. He was a former assistant attorney general and the recently appointed director of the FBI, Nelson Gramm.

"Director," Stone said, shaking the man's hand. "Special Agent Ness." He waved them to seats. "How may I help you?"

"First of all," Gramm said, "I want to thank you for your assistance in Hawaii and on the return flight."

"You're welcome."

"I would like to charter your airplane," Gramm said.

"With all the government aircraft available? Why?"

"There are certain expenditures that I have the authority to authorize immediately. The use of government aircraft is not one of them. That would require an official request, which would then filter down to an actionable level, and it could take a week or more."

"For what purpose do you wish to charter it?"

"To fly to the Sultanate of Saud and arrest Viktor Zanian."

Stone looked at Brio, who could not hold his gaze.

"Where did you get the information that Zanian is in the Sultanate?"

"From you. It seems that you are getting better information than we, and faster. We also wish to employ you as a consultant."

"And when do you want to fly to the Sultanate?"

"Now."

"Let me tell you what is involved in arranging this flight," Stone said.

"Please do."

"First of all, the charter fee will be twenty thousand dollars an hour, which begins at wheels up and ends at touchdown. The airplane requires two flight crews and two flight attendants: that's six people, and the charter fee does not include fuel, but I'll throw in catering. You'll need someone aboard with a valid credit card and a high credit limit for the fuel."

Brio raised her hand, then put it back in her lap.

"How many people do you wish to transport?"

"Two: Special Agent Ness and you."

"And the two of us are expected to penetrate whatever security Zanian and his host have?"

"I have authorized a team of eighteen agents, which will be

assembled from four of our European stations and will board in Cairo."

"So, we're just supposed to serve an arrest warrant and take him away?"

"Pretty much."

"Has anyone inquired of the sultan as to his feelings on the subject of Zanian?"

"That will be your job."

"I'm just supposed to drop my law practice, fly across the Atlantic Ocean and the Arabian Desert, and say, 'Please, sir, may I arrest your houseguest and take him away?'"

"I spoke with your managing partner, Bill Eggers, less than an hour ago, and he said we could do with you as we will, at a thousand dollars an hour."

"Sort of like being sold into bondage," Stone said.

"Only with your agreement."

"And why do you think I have enough sway with the sultan to pull this off? I've never met the man."

"He asked for you. He apparently read something about you in some magazine and was impressed. He called Lance Cabot for a reference."

Stone looked at Brio again. Now she was contemplating her lap.

"And Special Agent Ness has something she'd like to say to you," Gramm said.

Stone looked at Brio again. "Oh?"

She managed to raise her gaze a few degrees. "I wish to apologize for any doubts I may have had about your credentials and your acquaintances," she said.

"How very nice of you," Stone said sweetly. "Now, Director Gramm, I have to reassemble my crew, who need some rest after our last adventure, and have the aircraft inspected before a long flight, so the earliest we will be able to depart will be noon tomorrow."

"No earlier? We don't know how long Zanian will be in the Sultanate."

"Why would he want to leave?" Stone asked. "He just got there."

"Done," the director said, getting to his feet and offering his hand.

"I'll get my luggage," Brio said.

"Since we're not leaving until tomorrow, just leave it with Joan, and we'll take it with us to the airplane. Please be here at nine AM tomorrow."

"Thank you," she said, shooting him a dirty look. Then she followed her boss out of the office.

He called Faith and got the wheels turning.

"Have you ever flown into the Sultanate?" he asked.

"I've flown into Riad and Dubai, but never into the Sultanate of Saud. I don't expect it will be any more difficult than the other two."

Stone called Lance.

"I understand you're traveling tomorrow," Lance said.

"Anything you can do to pave the way would be appreciated by all."

"I'll see what I can do," Lance said, then hung up.

S tone slid into a booth with Dino and Viv at Patroon. "Welcome home, Viv," he said, kissing her on the cheek.

"Thank you, Stone. I guess I have you to thank for Dino's tan."

"I couldn't keep him out of the sun."

"I hear you're off again tomorrow," Dino said.

"Why is it you and everyone else knows about my travel plans before I do?"

"It's our job," Viv said.

"Have you ever been to the Sultanate of Saud?" Stone asked.

"Once," she said. "I've issued fly-around orders to all our flight crews."

"What is the place like?"

Viv stared at the ceiling for a moment. "Quaint," she said.

"That's all you've got? 'Quaint'?"

"I want to be as complimentary as I can."

"How's the food?"

"Just great, if you enjoy goat and, in a pinch, camel."

"I should think it would be wasteful to eat camels, when they're so useful."

"They have become less so, since the advent of Land Rovers," she said, "and they only eat them when they're very old. If I were you, I'd stick with the goat."

"What's that like?"

"It's like goat," she said. "It's good if they use enough garlic. Oh, by the way, the men all reek of garlic. It's like in Spain. If they eat enough garlic it gets into the bloodstream, then they emit."

"Any good local restaurants?"

"I'd stick to room service if I were you. And the only good place to stay is the palace."

"The Palace Hotel?"

"The palace. Where the sultan, his harem, and large numbers of his sons and other family live."

"And if we're not invited to stay?"

"Either get invited, or sleep on your airplane."

"What is the climate like this time of year?"

"Not to put too fine a point on it, hot."

"And the evenings?"

"Cold. Take a coat for the evenings."

"Any local shopping?"

"Yes, if you're looking to buy a camel or a goat. They sell them on the street corners."

"I think I'll pass on the shopping."

"Good idea."

"What's the local currency?"

"Dollars or euros. Don't take anything else, and don't accept the local currency as change. Deal in round numbers."

"Credit cards?"

"You may be able to buy aviation fuel with them. For everything else, think cash. It would be wise to take along a pile of it, since everyone expects a bribe."

"For what?"

"For anything they can think of. How long are you staying?"

"As short a time as possible."

"Nothing happens quickly in the Sultanate, and I mean *nothing*. If you're staying more than overnight, you should take along two—no, three hundred thousand dollars in cash."

"What service could be worth that kind of money?"

"How much is your airplane worth to you?"

"I'm going to have to buy it back from them?"

"It won't be as bad as that, but it will *seem* as bad. I've heard of one instance where a CEO returned to his private jet to find an engine missing. He had to pay for a new one, even though it was the one they had removed."

"I think I'll take a mechanic with us."

"And an engine."

"Oh, come on, Viv, it can't be as bad as that?"

"I told you, it will *seem* as bad."

Stone turned to Dino, who had been silent. "Can I borrow a platoon of your uniformed officers to guard the airplane?"

"You'll run up a big bill at the airport, if you do that," Viv said. "You'll need to bribe customs officials to get them in and out of the country."

"I was kidding," he said to Dino.

"Viv wasn't," Dino replied.

Stone got out his phone and called Brio Ness.

"Is everything all right?"

"Sort of. I've just been reliably informed that we should take a large amount of dollars to pay bribes on the ground."

"Whatever," she said.

"I'm told the bribes can be shocking, and God knows what we're going to have to pay for Zanian."

"What sort of money are we talking about?"

"I've been told to take three hundred thousand dollars for bribes. We may need a million to pay for Zanian."

"I'll call you back," she said, then hung up.

"How'd she take it?"

"She's calling her director."

Stefan, the maître d', was finishing his dance with the Caesar salad when Brio called back.

"I've arranged for a million three in cash," she said. "It will be delivered to the airplane tomorrow. Where is it?"

"Jet Aviation, at Teterboro. There's a safe on the airplane. I'm surprised you got permission so quickly."

"The director says we'll find a way to take it out of Zanian's hide."

"I'll bring you a contract to sign," Stone said.

"And I'll bring a receipt for you to sign." She hung up.

"She's bringing a million three," he said.

"From the FBI?"

"Directly from the director."

"I don't believe it."

"The director says he'll get it back from Zanian."

"And what if you don't get Zanian back?"

"We'd better," Stone said.

Viv spoke up, "What if you can't afford him?"

S tone called Lance.

"Yeess," Lance drawled.

"I need a briefing from somebody who knows the sultan well?"

"I understood you were briefed last evening at dinner."

"Viv is a pessimist. I'd like the advice of someone more, ah, cheerful."

"What do you want to know?"

"She tells me we should bring along a large sum of cash for bribes, and that we may have to pay as much as a million dollars, in cash, to get our hands on Zanian."

"Perhaps you should take your checkbook, as well."

Stone ignored that. "What is your personal advice about dealing with the sultan?"

"Keep your hand on your wallet. And your checkbook. At all times."

"What do you mean, 'At all times'?"

"Sleep with those items on your person, and sleep lightly. Beware of any female companionship offered."

"Should I take a weapon?"

"Only if you wish to donate it to the sultan's personal collection."

"What kind of negotiator is the sultan?"

"A demanding one. You must remember, Stone, that the man is an absolute monarch when in his own country. Memorize the cell number of the ambassador"—he recited it for Stone to copy down—"and do not hesitate to use it. He is the only person in the Sultanate who can threaten the sultan with the loss of American largesse."

"Anything else?"

"Did I mention, watch your ass?"

"Sort of."

"There is a dungeon in the nether regions of the royal palace. You do not wish to visit it, even for a moment."

"If I get into trouble, Lance, may I rely on you for help?"

"Help? If the sultan should take it into his mind to have you beheaded in his private courtyard, you can die screaming my name, and it will avail you nothing. I must run now. Good luck!" Lance hung up.

Stone hung up, too, thought for a moment, then he dialed a number in the 202 zip code. There was no answer. He dialed another number.

"White House switchboard," a woman's voice answered.

"This is Stone Barrington. I would like to speak to the president, if I may."

"One moment, Mr. Barrington."

It was a long moment before he heard the voice again. "I'm putting you through," she said.

"Good morning," she said.

"I'm sorry about going through the switchboard," he said. "Your cell didn't answer, and it's important."

"Stand by," she replied, then hung up.

Stone stood by nervously. Finally, his cell phone rang. The caller ID read, Private.

"Hello?"

"I have about six minutes. Is that enough?"

"Thank you, Holly, I hope so. I need your help in order to avoid being beheaded."

"Ah, you're visiting my dear friend the sultan, aren't you? I heard something about that."

"The rumors are true. The FBI wants me to go over there, arrest Zanian, and bring him back. I'm afraid the sultan may take exception to that."

"To the extent of having you beheaded? Really?"

"It would be of great help to me in accomplishing this if the sultan could be made to believe that you take a personal interest in my well-being, down to, and including, my fingers, toes, and neck. And genitalia."

"Well, we wouldn't want anything to happen to any of those, now would we?"

"Tell me, is there something that you were going to give the sultan anyway that I could present to him, in your stead? Something like a squadron of jet fighters, perhaps."

"I think what he really wants is a couple dozen Jeep Grand Cherokees," she said. "He's been having trouble with his Land Rovers because he doesn't take care of them. I believe that there may be no words in his dialect that translate as 'periodic servicing by a dealer.'"

"May I convey this gift on your behalf?"

"Hang on, I'll ask the chairman of the Joint Chiefs." She held her hand over the phone, and her words were muffled. Then she came back. "Oh, all right," she said. "The sultan will want to know when, and if he does, you are to tell him, 'In due course.' Nothing more."

"That's wonderful, thank you."

"And Stone, a couple of things to remember. When you are ushered into the presence, give him no salaams. Remember, you are a United States citizen, and we do not bow to royalty. Nothing more than a head nod."

"Right."

"Oh, one other thing: it is important, no matter what he says, to show no fear."

"Even to an absolute monarch who can have me beheaded?"

"Especially to him. Now, I must go and deal with the Pentagon. Good luck to you. I'll make our ambassador there, Henry Wilcox, aware of your coming presence."

"Thank you, Holly," he said, but she had already hung up.

Stone riffled through his memory to gather what tools he had at his disposal. It was precious little.

41

Stone packed two cases and a small trunk, more than he normally took, but in order to be ready for anything, he had to take along a morning suit, with a collapsible top hat, waistcoat, striped trousers, a wing-collared shirt, and a silk cravat. Also, a chalk-striped dark blue suit, two linen suits, four pairs of shoes, and enough shirts to sweat through three a day, and a dinner jacket and two pleated dress shirts.

He also took along his trench coat, with a buttoned-in cashmere lining, lined gloves, and a long cashmere scarf, and finally, a tweed hat.

He called Brio and briefed her on his conversations and to warn her of the chilly evenings. "You need not worry about overpacking, since we don't have to check our luggage. Do you have a diplomatic passport?"

"In the works," she said. "I'm glad you're taking this seriously, but really, Stone!"

"Your lord and master said something about eighteen FBI agents boarding in Cairo. I hope he wasn't talking about boarding *my* airplane."

"I understand, and I believe they're using another government aircraft. They'll join us in the air near Cairo, contact us on the radio and follow us in."

"Did somebody caution you about not, ah, curtseying?"

"What?"

"We are American citizens, and we don't bow to royalty. There's nothing to stop you from flashing your cleavage at the sultan, though."

"Oh gee, thanks."

"Did anybody tell you about the dungeon under the royal palace?"

"Oh, come on."

"And what's the line from the movie? Nobody can hear you scream."

"I'm beginning to wish I hadn't invited you along."

"'Invited me'? That was an invitation? I regret accepting, more and more each hour."

"The million in cash will be in a leather suitcase, and the other three hundred grand in a matching valise, both from the confiscated evidence room in the Hoover building. The property clerk swears it's Dillinger's luggage."

"If we run short of cash, maybe we can auction it off on the Internet."

"I can't think of anything else," she said.

"Me, too. Goodbye." He hung up and buzzed Joan.

"Yes, sir?"

"How much ready cash do we keep in my checking account?" he asked.

"At least a hundred grand."

"Tomorrow, stoke it with a million on top of that, and give me the wire transfer info."

"It's on every check in your checkbook."

"And warn the bank to pay *any* sum I write a check for or ask to be wired."

"What in the world are you going to buy?"

"A fugitive felon, I hope." He hung up and thought about the dungeon. Maybe I should pack some long underwear, he thought.

Stone was on the airplane on time, and the flight attendant pointed at two old-fashioned pieces of luggage. "Those just arrived," she said, and held up some keys. "These will open them."

Stone set the larger case on a seat, unlocked it, and opened it. Hundreds and fifties. There was a pouch inside the case, as well. Stone opened it, stuffed his .380, the silencer, and three magazines inside and rebuttoned it, then locked the case again.

He made the same inspection of the accompanying valise, then relocked it.

What had he forgotten?

"Have you forgotten anything?" Brio asked from behind him.

"I brought everything," he said.

"Separate transport is confirmed for my agents."

"You'd better let them know that they're not going to get into the palace with weapons. They should leave them on the airplane, but accessible. The agents are going to have to remain in reserve, too. We can't arrive at the palace with eighteen bulky men. The sultan will suspect something."

"They're not going to like that in the least," she said.

"Nothing I can do about it. Same goes for you, my dear. And strapping it to your inner thigh is just going to invite an invasion of your person."

Faith walked back to where they were taking their seats, and beckoned Stone to join her.

"What is it?"

"I know this is going to sound strange, but there is no international airport in the Sultanate of Saud."

"So, where are we going to land? In Riad, then drive eight hundred miles to the palace?"

"I've been given coordinates and a radio frequency. I'll enter the longitude and latitude into the GPS and hope for the best, I suppose."

"Make sure we have fuel to a reasonable alternate."

"I have already done so."

"Oh, as we pass Cairo, we're going to pick up an escort, or rather, a tail. It's another airplane with eighteen FBI agents aboard. They'll contact you, and you can give them the location. I don't know how I'm going to explain them to the sultan. And by the way, I think that, since we're uncertain of our accommodations, you and your crew had better bunk aboard. It will be cold at night, but you'll need the AC in the daytime."

"I hope there's hangar space available wherever we're going," she said.

"We may just have to make do."

"I hope we don't get a sandstorm, then. That would remove your paint job."

"That's what insurance is for," Stone replied.

Or rather, the FBI, he thought.

They took off for Cairo. Faith had chosen that for her fuel stop, so that she could arrive at their destination with plenty of fuel for a long flight out if anything went wrong.

They landed at Cairo and refueled without incident. Faith was approached by three men in airline uniforms, and they pointed out their aircraft, a Dassault French jet with three engines. Its passengers could be seen to be boarding.

Faith returned to the Gulfstream. "One of those in the pilot's uniforms is our agent in charge of the operation."

"I thought you were AIC," Stone said to Brio.

"I am. Think of me as the super AIC."

"Right."

Faith said, "I've shared the coordinates of our destination with them, and they'll take off fifteen minutes after we do and maintain that distance. We'll be in constant radio contact. They understand that, should they enter the palace, they should go unarmed." She handed Brio a handheld radio. "This will keep you in touch with them. It has a range of a few miles."

Brio tucked it into a pocket of the jumpsuit she was wearing.

"I don't think you should dress that way for entrance into the palace," Stone said. "The sultan and his people would find it disrespectful."

"Don't worry, I'll change before we land."

"What's our flight time?" Stone asked Faith.

"About three hours." She took out a chart and showed them how their destination had been marked with an X. "Middle of nowhere," she said, "and it's a big desert, as you will see. Our route calls for us to take off and fly along the route of the Suez Canal, then turn inland at altitude, which will be FL 280, so you'll have a view, of sorts."

"Let's do it, then," Stone said, with more enthusiasm than he felt.

They had dinner, then tried to get some sleep. When Stone awoke, the sunrise had turned the sky red, and they were flying lower than he had expected. The air was crystal clear, and there was nothing but the Arabian Desert as far as the eye could see. The terrain and its emptiness inspired awe. The intercom buzzed.

"Yes?"

"Good news," Faith said. "Our destination has an instrument landing system to guide us in. We're descending now."

Stone looked outside the window until they touched softly down, but saw only sand and stone. As the airplane slowed to taxi speed and made a turn he saw a large grove of palm trees, with a cluster of spires rising above them. The airplane came to a stop, and the engines shut down, but the APU continued to supply power and air-conditioning.

Brio, having changed into a modest, dark dress, was looking out windows on the opposite side of the aircraft. "Do you see anyone?"

Stone checked his window again. "There's a cloud of dust," he said. "Looks like men on horseback and camels."

Faith let down the airstairs door, and before anyone could exit a man in an arab headdress and robes over white trousers entered. "Good day! I am Colonel Said of the Royal Mounted Corps. I am to transport you to the royal palace."

"On camels?" Brio asked.

"No, madam. We have brought Range Rovers for you and your luggage. You are Madam Ness of the FBI, are you not?"

"I am," she replied. "How do you do?"

"Very well, thank you." Then he turned toward Stone. "And you are Mr. Stone Barrington, are you not?"

"I am. How do you do?"

"Still very well, thank you."

Faith had appeared, and he asked her to point out the luggage so his men could take care of it.

Shortly, they were in a slightly worn Range Rover, driving rapidly toward the grove of palm trees. Stone could not see a road, as such, but their way was smooth. Once among the palm trees men, horses, camels, and other vehicles appeared.

"This is the Saud Oasis," announced Colonel Said. "One of the largest in the whole of the Arabian Desert. You will be at the palace shortly."

The palace appeared as a dream, a collection of brightly colored spires floating inside a high wall. "How old is the palace?" Stone asked Colonel Said.

"It dates from the twelfth century but has been rebuilt many times since that day. I am told that another aircraft has landed on our field. Whom does it contain?"

Brio spoke up, "Special agents of the FBI, who will assist us in our work and depart at the same time we do. They will not require food or lodging overnight."

"I see. Are they armed?"

"Yes, with the standard weapons of our service. They are not hostile. They are merely here to protect us."

"I will explain this to the sultan in such a way that he will not order them shot and their aircraft burned."

"Thank you," Brio said.

He led them into the palace, which was cooler inside than Stone had expected.

"Your quarters are adjacent to each other," the colonel said softly to Stone. "For your convenience."

Stone nodded but said nothing in response. "What power source does the palace operate on?" he asked.

"There is an oil field nearby, which meets all our needs, but we are beginning to install solar equipment, as well."

They came to a large pair of double doors, behind which lay a vestibule, with doors leading off two sides. Said directed Ness to be led to one, while he led Stone to the other.

The room was very large, perhaps forty feet in length, and there was much gilt and red in the décor. The bed was larger than an American king-sized one, and a box of switches rested on a bedside table.

"Here are lights and American satellite TV," Said said, flipping switches. Flipping one of them caused a very large TV set to rise from the floor at the foot of the bed.

Stone was shown a large, well-stocked bathroom and a seating area in the bedroom with a cluster of sofas and chairs before a large gas fireplace.

"Your clothing will be delivered, pressed, presently, but there are two cases that are locked, one large, one small."

"Those contain gifts for the sultan, which I will present at a later time," he said.

"Do they contain any explosives?" Said asked.

"Certainly not," Stone replied. "Everything inside is for the amusement of the sultan."

"Very well. Someone will come to escort you to dinner at seven o'clock. The dress will be black tie." They coordinated their watches. "Your clothes will be here shortly." He bowed, then left the room.

There was a knock on an interior door, and Brio appeared. She walked toward the bed and beckoned Stone to follow her. "Have you noticed this?" She leaned over the bed and pointed up at the canopy above. Stone followed her finger and saw that a mirror, as large as the bed, hung above.

"It would seem that the sultan has provided for our every entertainment," Stone said.

"It would not surprise me to learn that the suite is equipped with cameras and microphones," Brio said.

"Oh, good," Stone replied. "We can watch ourselves later."

43

tone napped a little, and at six o'clock there was a rap on the door. "Come!" Stone shouted.

A valet pushed a cart into the room. There was a rack where Stone's clothes hung and another at the bottom, containing his personal luggage. Everything was put away. Stone very nearly tipped the man but reconsidered. Who knew what the local custom was?

There was a bottle of Knob Creek in among his shirts and underwear, and he thought of having a drink, since, in a Muslim society, he was not likely to be offered one later. Instead, he had a soak in his large tub, then he shaved, showered, and got dressed in his dinner suit. After some thought, he unlocked the trunk, removed his pistol and holster, and put them in his briefcase, then he relocked the trunk.

At precisely seven o'clock, the colonel returned and collected

Stone and Brio and led them for a bit of a walk through the palace. It was more elegant and in better repair than Stone had anticipated. They were finally admitted to an indoor garden space with a ceiling height of about forty feet. An area like a living room had been set in its midst.

Two men stood in the middle of the room, one a Westerner dressed as Stone was, but with gray hair and horn-rimmed glasses. The other wore an evening suit with a silk brocade jacket of a floral design; he had iron-gray hair and a Vandyke beard and mustache.

The colonel spoke, "Your Majesty, may I present Ms. Brio Ness of the Federal Bureau of Investigation and Mr. Stone Barrington of the law firm of Woodman & Weld. Mr. Barrington is also an associate director of the Central Intelligence Agency. Mr. Barrington, may I present His Majesty, the Sultan of Saud and the Honorable Henry Wilcox, ambassador to His Majesty from the United States of America."

Stone and Brio both executed a slight head bow and a how do you do. Wilcox shook both their hands. The sultan stood with his hands behind him.

"I am very sure that each of you would like a drink," the sultan said, with an English accent born at Eton. "My imam has declared this room neutral territory in that regard."

They both assented. Brio asked for a dry martini, and Stone was handed a glass of Knob Creek without asking for it.

The sultan accepted a whiskey, too, and the ambassador had one already clenched in his fist.

Glasses were raised.

"The president of the United States," the sultan said, and a drink was taken.

"The Sultan of Saud," the ambassador said in return, and they drank again. Then things became more relaxed.

"I hope your travel here was not a punishment," the sultan said.

"We were very comfortable," Brio replied.

"Ah, yes, in Mr. Barrington's beautiful Gulfstream."

"Which I am fortunate to have," Stone replied, with as much modesty as he could muster.

"I also admired the FBI's choice in aircraft," the sultan said. "I once owned such an airplane. It was very nice, but it was not a Gulfstream. They are in a class by themselves. I once toured their factory in Savannah, Georgia, and was impressed with their attention to every detail. If I were not an honorable man, I would confiscate your airplane."

Everyone chuckled at the mere suggestion that the sultan might not be an honorable man.

"Mr. Barrington," the sultan said, "I am told that you have come bearing gifts."

"I have, sir. Perhaps we can find a more opportune time later in the evening for me to present them?"

"As you wish, Mr. Barrington." He smiled at them all. "Now I am beginning to think that this may be more a business meeting, than merely a social one."

"I hope that the sultan may find it a pleasant transaction," Stone said.

"I have been reading up on Mr. Barrington," the sultan said, "and he has led a fascinating life."

"Only because I have the good fortune to meet such fascinating people," Stone said, raising his glass in the sultan's direction.

"My condolences on the loss of your beautiful wife, Arrington," the sultan said.

"Thank you, Your Majesty. She is greatly missed by our son and me."

"Ah, yes, your son, Peter, the film director. I have ordered his films, but they have yet to arrive."

"Had I known of Your Majesty's interest, I would have brought them to you. I shall see that their delivery is expedited."

The sultan beamed. "I shall look forward to receiving them. I am disappointed, I must say, not to meet your good friend, New York's Commissioner of Police Bacchetti, who I was told is your constant companion."

"A frequent companion, certainly," Stone replied, "but not a constant one. The commissioner has a wife and job, both of which occupy much of his time."

"And Ms. Ness," the sultan said. "There are rumors that you will soon become an assistant director of your organization."

"As we say in America, Your Majesty, from your lips to God's ear."

The sultan laughed uproariously.

"I am very taken with your garden," she said.

"Come, and let me show you some rare plantings," the sultan said.

Brio set down her glass and took his offered hand.

"If you would excuse us, gentlemen." They walked, arm in arm, into the garden.

The ambassador faced Stone. "I must say, this is all going very well. I was afraid I would have to intercede to keep the conversation light."

"You may have to yet, Ambassador," Stone said.

"Please call me Henry."

"Of course, Henry. May I question you on a point of diplomacy and gift-giving?"

"Of course."

Stone explained what he had in mind.

"Well," Wilcox said. "I don't see why not. It's no skin off the nation's nose, after all."

The sultan returned with Brio, and they were called to dinner.

As Brio brushed past Stone, she said, "The old dog propositioned me."

"Careful that you don't end up in his harem," Stone replied.

After more conversation, but no discussion about Stone's mission, they were escorted behind a hedge of ferns, where an elaborately set dinner table rested: tableware and goblets of gold, and two bottles of claret—Château Mouton Rothschild, '61—stood beside decanters that had received the wine. The center of the table was occupied by a large, roasted fowl, decorated with a peacock's fantail.

A servant expertly carved the bird, nearly the size of a turkey, and distributed the plates, finished with a risotto and fresh *petit poi*. The sultan tasted the wine and signaled his approval. Stone approved, too. It was a rare treat. Stone thought the bird delicious, and he was relieved that it didn't have a hump.

When they had finished and drunk both bottles of wine, crêpes Grand Marnier were served, along with a Château d'Yquem, '59—the finest dessert wine of Bordeaux.

After dinner, port—a Quinto de Nationale, '29—was passed to the left in a Baccarat decanter, and a perfect Stilton accompanied it.

"Your Majesty," Stone said, raising his glass, "I have never experienced a more perfect repast, nor had a feeling of more perfect contentment, than at your table. On behalf of all your guests, I thank you." There were "Hear, hears" all around.

The sultan beamed at them. "Nor have I had more perfect guests." Then his face changed, and Stone was not pleased by what he saw there. "Now, to business," he said. The sultan turned his head and nodded at his colonel, who stepped into the garden and returned, not alone.

Stone heard a sound that immediately made him think of the Ghost of Christmas Past, from Dickens—the sound of chains being dragged over stone. He looked up to see a frowning man in a wrinkled and dirty suit with a collar around his neck, and his wrists and ankles shackled.

"May I present Mr. Viktor Zanian," the sultan said.

The colonel poked the man in the ribs with a bejeweled dagger.

"How do you do?" Zanian said.

"I regret that you must meet the gentleman in reduced circumstances," the sultan said, "but he did not dine on peacock and French wines this evening."

Stone reflected that he appeared not to have dined at all, looking gaunt and shrunken.

"Now," the sultan said. "What am I offered?"

It took Stone a moment to understand that he was referring to Zanian.

Brio was quicker. "On behalf of the United States Government," she said, "I will take him off your hands."

"Once again," the sultan said. "What am I offered?"

"A quarter of a million dollars," Brio replied.

"I fear that Mr. Zanian is a more expensive commodity than that," the sultan replied.

"Your Majesty," Henry Wilcox said, "I ask you to remember that Ms. Ness is a civil servant and does not have access to great wealth."

"Well, then," the sultan said. "Perhaps Mr. Barrington can improve on her offer."

"Your Majesty," Stone said, "I would not insult your throne by bargaining with you over a criminal. Instead, I will simply offer you everything at my disposal: two million dollars, if your servant will bring my large case." Moments later, the trunk was wheeled to the table. Stone unlocked and opened it. The cash smiled back at them.

"I am grateful for your offer," the sultan said, "although it lacks a certain flair."

"But I have not finished," Stone said. "If you will permit me to continue."

"But of course," the sultan replied, with a wave of his hand.

"I also bring you, with the personal compliments of the president of the United States, a fleet of twenty-four Jeep Grand Cherokees."

The sultan's eyebrows shot up, and he smiled. "To be delivered when?"

"In due course," Stone replied.

The sultan's smile vanished.

Henry Wilcox stood. "Your Majesty," he said. "The fleet now reposes in two large aircraft at the airport in Riyadh, and they will depart for the Sultanate of Saud at your command."

The sultan beamed again. "Mr. Barrington, your country's offer is accepted. Where would you like Mr. Zanian placed?"

"Aboard our second airplane, Your Majesty, where he will be secured."

"It shall be done immediately," the sultan said, motioning to the colonel, who went for Zanian and rushed him out of the building.

The ambassador produced a cell phone and pressed a button. "You are authorized to fly to the Sultanate of Saud," he said, then hung up. "The automobiles are on their way and will be here by sunrise."

"All is well, then," the sultan replied. "And now, if you will forgive me, I shall retire for the night. Mr. Barrington, Ms. Ness, it has been my great pleasure to entertain you. Your luggage awaits you on Mr. Barrington's airplane."

Stone and Brio were escorted from the palace and into a Range Rover.

"That was swift," Brio said.

"I've no complaint with that," Stone said. "I want to get out of here before the sultan changes his mind on some whim or other."

45

Stone, Brio, and Henry Wilcox arrived at the airfield to see no one in sight. After a moment, two men dressed in military desert fatigues departed the FBI aircraft and trotted over to their car, as Stone and Brio got out.

"Ness," one of them said, handing her a folded sheet of paper, "a personal message for you from the director." She read it and smiled, then handed it to Stone, who read it aloud.

My dear Brio,

Congratulations on the success of your mission. It is my pleasure to promote you to the post of assistant director for Criminal Investigations. I look forward to seeing you and your arrestee in New York.

"Congratulations," Stone said, kissing her on the cheek.

"And my congratulations, too," Wilcox echoed.

"Forgive me if I blush becomingly," she said.

"Is our mission complete?" the FBI agent asked.

"As long as our perpetrator has been secured aboard your airplane," Brio replied.

The agent looked puzzled. "Ma'am?"

"I believe Colonel Said delivered Viktor Zanian to you a few minutes ago."

The man looked slightly ill. "No, ma'am," he replied. "We haven't seen either of them."

"Did someone arrive here in a Range Rover?" Stone asked.

"Yes, sir," the man said. "They drove into the big hangar over there, and after a few minutes, they came out in some sort of half-track desert vehicle and drove away."

Stone and Brio were struck dumb for a moment.

"In which direction?" Stone asked.

The man pointed down the runway. "Thataway."

"In which direction is Saudi Arabia?" Stone asked.

"That way, to the north," the man replied.

"Well," Stone said, "he won't go there. He wouldn't get a friendly welcome." Stone got a map of the country out of his briefcase and flattened it on the back of the other agent as Faith walked up.

"Faith, where is the nearest major airport, south of us?"

Faith looked at the map, then tapped a finger on it. "Dubai," she said, "right there on the Persian Gulf, to the ESE. Are we thinking of our Gulfstream?"

"I'm thinking more of Zanian's Gulfstream, and where he

might have left it. Maybe we can cut him off there since he's traveling through the desert."

The ambassador spoke up. "We've no assurance that he's gone to Dubai," he said. "We might be better off tracking him on the ground."

"In what?" Stone asked, looking around at the airport. "There's only the one Range Rover, the one they left in the hangar."

"There are no keys in it," the FBI agent said. "We looked, and none of us knows how to hot-wire a Range Rover."

"Let me make a call," Wilcox said, taking out his cell phone and walking a few feet away. He returned shortly. "Ten minutes," he said. "We might as well get our luggage out of the sultan's car." With the help of some FBI agents, they unloaded the car and stacked the luggage beside it. Stone saw his trunk and his valise among them.

"Please keep a close watch on these two pieces," he said to the FBI man. "Their contents are valuable."

The man turned to Brio. "Ma'am? Is that all right with you?"

"Oh, yes," she said. "The contents of that trunk belong to the FBI."

"But not the valise," Stone said. "Unless we lose it, then it's all yours."

The man didn't seem to understand, but he assigned another agent to watch the luggage.

"There comes our transport," Wilcox said, pointing to the north.

"That's big," Faith said.

"It's a C-17 Globemaster," Wilcox said, "and there are two of them, each containing twelve Jeep Grand Cherokees."

"We're going to steal the sultan's Jeeps?" Stone asked. "I understand he removes peoples' heads for less serious offenses."

"They are still the property of the United States Government," Wilcox said, "until I turn them over to the sultan, and I have not yet done so."

Shortly, the two giant aircrafts were on the ground, and after a conversation with the commander of the flight, the armed military crews—with the help of the FBI agents—began unloading the cars, while the FBI agents moved their luggage, weapons, and many cases of water to the Jeeps.

"They're dealer-prepped, gassed up," the commander said, "and ready to go, Ambassador. And they have the GPS map software for this part of the world."

Finally, they were ready. "I've been out here for five years," Wilcox said, "so I'm generally familiar with the area." He used Stone's map, spread on the hood of a Jeep. "Just about here, too small to be on your map, is an oasis called Ben Hur, named after the movie. It's likely Zanian and Said will head there, since it's the last stop for fuel and water for a long time. Fortunately, there's a road, so we don't have to go over land." He entered the Ben Hur name in the GPS, and the map popped up. "Here it is, so let's get going."

"How fast can that half-track go?" Brio asked.

"Over open territory, they'd have a big advantage, but not on a road," Wilcox said. "We may be able to outrun them."

"Let's find out," Stone said.

Brio turned to her FBI agent. "Report only to me," she said, "not to the director. I'll do that myself." She got into a Jeep with Stone and Wilcox, who took the shotgun seat, so that he could operate the GPS.

"You're not keeping the director updated?" Stone asked her.

"No, I want to be an assistant director of the FBI, at least for a little while." She got on her handheld radio and confirmed that she was communicating with the other Jeeps.

Stone put the car into gear and followed Wilcox's directions. Shortly, they were on some sort of road, with twenty-three Jeeps, all painted a gleaming white, strung out behind them.

46

There were places where the road was pretty much obliterated by the shifting sands of the desert, but mostly, he felt he could drive at seventy mph in safety. They were comfortable in their seatbelts and with the vehicle's air-conditioning on.

"The Jeeps are configured with special ACs for the desert," Wilcox said. "I know because I configured them. The cooling systems are beefed up."

"That's comforting to know," Stone said. He put on his sunglasses, as did the others. "Brio, call your guys on the radio and ask them to keep an eye out for that half-track."

"I don't think they would drive it on the road," Wilcox said. "The noise of the tracks on asphalt would be intolerable."

"I'll bet they're following the road," Stone said. "I mean, they're not going to be using celestial navigation. They'll use the GPS, just like us."

Brio made the call to the other cars.

"When we refuel at the oasis," Brio said, "I hope they take credit cards."

"Why?" Stone asked. "When we've got two and a quarter million dollars in cash in the trunk."

"Why didn't Zanian take it with him?"

"They were in a big hurry. Maybe they just forgot to transfer the trunk to the half-track."

Another hour of driving, and Stone pointed. "Is that a mirage? I see palm trees."

"That's the real thing," Wilcox said. They drove into the palms, and at the direction of Henry Wilcox, found the pumps, in what looked like an ordinary service station.

Wilcox got out of the Jeep and conversed in Arabic with the attendant. He pointed at all the Jeeps.

The man looked at them in consternation. Wilcox said, "He says he hopes he has enough gasoline, but he's joking. He also says his tanks were filled by fuel trucks yesterday."

"Does he take credit cards?"

Wilcox asked him and the man nodded assent.

"Ask him if he's seen the half-track," Stone said, and Wilcox did so. Wilcox came back to the car. "He says the half-track was filled more than an hour ago, then drove back in the direction of the airfield we just left."

"He's remembered the trunk," Stone said, "and he's going back for it. Brio, radio everybody to return to the airport when they've refueled, and to watch for the half-track along the way. They'll be armed and dangerous."

"Right," Brio said.

"How are your men armed?" Stone asked.

"With M-16 assault rifles and Beretta 9mm sidearms. Standard military issue. Ours are in the trunk."

"Let's get them into the cabin with us," Stone said.

After moving the weapons, while waiting for all twenty-four Jeeps to be refueled, Stone and Brio walked across the road to a little hillock and surveyed the view. It would be sunset soon, and that would make the half-track harder to find, unless they used their headlights.

"This is gorgeous," Brio said of the sunset.

"Yes," Stone said. "I wish we had a blanket and no FBI agents traveling with us."

She pinched him on the ass. "A one-track mind," she said.

Wilcox was taking a turn at the wheel, and Stone, now in the rear seat, got his phone out.

"Who are you calling?" Brio asked.

"Faith," he said. "No answer on her cell. I'll try the satphone." He dialed another number, and the copilot answered.

"Put Faith on," Stone said.

"Yes, I'm here. I can hear you on my headset."

"What's your location?"

"About an hour out of Dubai," she said.

"Go ahead and land there, and while you're refueling, see if Zanian's Gulfstream is at that airport."

"And if it isn't?"

"Return to the Sultanate because that's where his airplane is going to be repositioned to. They forgot something important and had to go back for it. You've got enough fuel to return to the Sultanate, and still make Cairo, haven't you?"

"Yes."

"Then don't refuel at Dubai. Wait and do it at the Sultanate."

"Okay, we'll just look for the Gulfstream, and then take off, if we don't find it."

"Let me know if you find it."

"Will do."

Stone hung up. "I've never played cat and mouse with twenty-four Jeeps and two Gulfstreams," he said.

"Thank God Zanian forgot the trunk," Brio said.

"I agree. He might be gone by now if he hadn't."

The group mounted up and made a U-turn back to where they came from.

An hour later, Faith called.

"Yes?"

"Stone, the airplane was at Dubai, but it left shortly after we landed."

"Where did they file for?"

"The coordinates of the Sultanate's airport."

"Okay, go flat out, and damn the fuel use. When you get there, whether the other airplane is there or not, park in the middle of the runway and leave the APU running and all the lights on, especially the wingtip strobes."

"Why?"

"Because if you get there first, I want to keep their Gulfstream from landing, and if you don't, I want to keep them from taking off. But listen, if they fire on you or threaten you, even with small arms, get out of their way. I don't want our airplane shot up."

"Got it." She hung up.

"You know," Brio said. "I really did underestimate you at the outset. I apologize. Just one thing, though."

"What's that?"

"Are you and the ambassador aware that you are both wearing tuxedos?"

"We do what we can with what we've got," Stone said.

s they approached the Sultanate's airport, Stone stopped about a mile out and looked ahead. "Anybody see any flashing lights?" he asked. It was dark now.

"No," the other occupants said.

"Open all the windows," he said, "and listen." They all listened.

"I hear something," Brio said.

Stone got out of the car and faced east, and the others followed. "Landing lights," Stone said pointing ahead of them.

Then a large aircraft flew over them at about five hundred feet, shaking them with the noise, and touched down on the runway, making a lot more noise as it reversed its engines. "That's a Gulfstream," Stone said.

"Yes," Brio said, "but which one?"

"I can't tell," Wilcox said.

"Neither can I," Stone echoed. "Brio, get on your horn and tell all the Jeeps to stay off the runway."

Brio did as she was asked. "What's happening?" she asked.

"We're waiting for the other Gulfstream," Stone said. "If it lands, it's ours, because the first one didn't block the runway."

They stood in the darkness and waited. A cloud moved, and the moon revealed itself, plump and full.

"That should make driving easier in the dark," Wilcox said.

Stone got Faith on the satphone. "What's your location?" he asked.

"Ten minutes out of the Sultanate airfield," she said.

"Another Gulfstream landed five minutes ago, and it's at the far end of the field. You perform a short field landing, stop in the center of the runway, do a 180-degree turn, stop, and shut down your engines, but keep the APU running and all lights on."

"Short field landing, one-eighty turn and stop, engines off, APU and lights on. Leave enough runway length to take off again."

"Why are you telling her that?" Brio asked.

"I don't want to end up with the two airplanes nose to nose. There is no reverse gear on an airplane, so they would both be stymied. I want our airplane to be able to take off again, if necessary."

"Okay, got it," Brio said.

Wilcox pointed East. "We've got lights. Airplane landing. It looks very low, perhaps too low."

"That's Faith aiming for the very end of the runway. Normally, she'd aim at the markings farther down, but she wants to stop short."

The airplane suddenly seemed to lose power.

"She's cut the engines," Stone said. "She's landing dead-stick."

"What's 'dead-stick'?" Brio asked.

"No power. She's turned a Gulfstream into a glider."

"How well do they glide?"

"Not well," Stone said.

The Gulfstream appeared, and set down on the runway, brakes screaming. Then, as it slowed, it swung right, almost stopped, swung left, completed the 180-degree turn, and stopped.

"Brilliant," Stone said.

"That's the scariest thing I've ever seen," Brio said.

"Everybody into the car," Stone said as he got behind the wheel and started the engine. "Brio, get on the horn and tell the Jeeps to line up across the runway behind our airplane, headlights on. I want them to be sure they're trapped."

Brio made the call, and the Jeeps started to move. Stone didn't join them but aimed at the open hangar across the runway.

"Where are you going?" Brio asked.

"To where they left the Range Rover, where they think the trunk is."

Brio handed two handguns forward and aimed an M-16 out a window and worked the action. Suddenly, Stone braked.

A lone vehicle sat there in the darkness.

"That's not a Range Rover," Wilcox said. "That's the half-track. They've switched to the Range Rover. Look." He pointed ahead toward the rear of the hangar.

Stone drove toward the rear doors and eased through the

narrow opening. Ahead of them was more of the moonlit Arabian Desert than Stone wanted to see. Far ahead, he saw two red lights, which suddenly disappeared. "There they go."

"Stop," Wilcox said, getting out his map. "How much fuel do you have left?"

"Less than half a tank."

"He's got a full tank in the Range Rover; it's been driven only from the palace. That's why they changed vehicles. You'll have to gas up, before we go after them, and you'd better bring a couple of full jerry cans, as well.

Stone drove around to the FBO office, now dark. He used his pistol to shoot the lock off the door. Inside, they ransacked the drawers, until they found the pump keys. They found some empty jerry cans, too, and filled three of them.

Meantime, Brio was on the horn to her agents. She ordered twelve cars to stay with the airplanes and prevent anyone from moving them and for the other twelve to fill their tanks and wait for further instructions.

Wilcox had a light on a desk and spread out his map. "They'll be headed west, toward Jeddah, on the Red Sea. Just before that is Makkah, a last-chance-for-fuel stop. There's nowhere else to go in that direction, and they can get out of Jeddah by boat, plane, or rail."

The two men changed from their tuxedos into desert clothing, while they waited for some of the Jeeps to refuel. Brio used the ladies' room to do the same. Stone called Faith and told her to have her crew get some dinner from the galley and to rest up. "We're headed for Jeddah," he said. "Flight plan for there and pick an FBO for refueling. You need to beat us there by at least an hour."

Finally, they were back in their Jeep and set off. What Jeeps had refueled followed them west.

"Now we're in Lawrence of Arabia country," Wilcox said.

48

They were back on the road, and a better one than the last. Stone was able to manage eighty mph at times, but he knew the Range Rover could do so as well.

"I wish I could sleep," Brio said from the rear seat.

"What's stopping you?" Stone asked, dodging a pothole.

"Ha!"

"That's okay. When it's your turn to drive, I won't be able to sleep, either."

An hour along Stone saw red lights far ahead. They were flashing, and they weren't moving.

"What is that?" Wilcox asked.

"There's a flashing blue light, too," Stone said, pointing. "It's got to be a police car. Maybe they're getting a ticket."

"What are we going to do, if we catch up to them?" Wilcox asked.

"Capture them or shoot them," Stone said. "There won't be another choice."

Now the stationary car seemed to be rushing at them. Stone slowed and pulled alongside, and Wilcox turned a flashlight on it.

"Two men, apparently dead," the diplomat said. "The windshield and the front windows are all shot out."

"I guess they didn't want to be arrested for speeding," Stone said, pulling ahead and switching off his headlights.

"Is there enough moonlight to drive this fast?" Brio asked.

"I hope so. Tell your people about the police car and tell them to shut off their headlights. I don't think we want them to see us coming."

"Not after that," Wilcox muttered.

"I wonder," Stone said, "if they looked for the trunk in the Range Rover when it was in the hangar, or just assumed it was there?"

"They might have assumed it if they were in a big enough hurry," Brio said.

They blew through the empty streets of a small village.

"Warn your Jeeps," Stone said to Brio. "We may have woken up some people."

Brio did as instructed.

Another two hours passed, and a glow appeared in the western sky. "That's the loom of Jeddah," Wilcox said, "and about on schedule."

"Where are we going to look for them once we're there?" Stone asked.

"The airport?" Wilcox asked. "I doubt if there'll be much flying this early. That will be true for Zanian's Gulfstream, too. Most airports don't open before seven or eight AM."

"Train station?"

"Same there. Not much moving."

"Waterfront?"

"That's a better choice, I think. Problem is, they could be in any kind of boat."

"What are the choices on the Red Sea?"

"Dhows, and plenty of them. Cargo ships. Tankers."

"Think private," Stone said. "Motor yachts?"

"There won't be much of that," Wilcox said. "Jeddah is more a commercial port than a place for pleasure cruising."

"If they can find a boat, where would they head for?" Stone asked.

"Alexandria or, more likely, Cairo," Wilcox replied. "They can get lost there, or Zanian's airplane can meet them."

They reached a road that ran along the edge of the Red Sea. Stone turned left and drove along for a few miles, and as he did, boats became scarcer. He made a U-turn.

"This looks more likely," Wilcox said. "There, there's a motor yacht."

"I think Zanian would be looking for something more comfortable," Stone said. He slowed as shops began to appear along the road. He passed one with a large sign that read: TRAVEL AGENT BOOK PASSAGE. CHARTER AIRCRAFT AND YACHTS. He looked at his watch. "Seven-thirty," he said.

"Aircraft taking off over yonder," Wilcox said, pointing. "Looks like a commercial flight."

There was a restaurant, a working-class sort of place, a couple doors down from the travel agent. "Let's get some breakfast while we wait for the travel place to open."

They parked and went inside, where they found a table and let Wilcox, with his Arabic, order for them. They got eggs and some sort of sausage, and a pot of coffee.

"Suppose Zanian makes Cairo?" Wilcox said. "Where would he likely go from there?"

"He wants to disappear, at least for a while, so not Rome, Paris, or London," Stone replied.

"How about Sicily?" Wilcox asked.

"Why Sicily?"

"Less crowded than bigger places this time of year. Decent airport, rental houses, a tradition of lawlessness on the part of some of the population."

"I like it, but it's a wild pitch," Stone said. Stone called Faith's cell phone and couldn't get connected. He tried the satphone and Faith answered.

"Hello?"

"Where are you?"

"Holding at the VOR," she replied. "Jeddah won't let us land yet. Maybe another half hour."

"Is Zanian's Gulfstream still back at the Sultanate's airport?"

"Yes, and we've got the runway blocked with half a dozen Jeeps, so they're not going anywhere soon."

"Call me back when you've had a look around the Jeddah airport."

"Will do." They both hung up.

"The airport is looking less likely for Zanian," Stone said. "Faith has got him boxed in, and she's waiting to land in Jeddah."

An hour later, the travel agent opened. As they walked into the office a lone woman in Western business clothes was tidying up.

"Good morning," she said, in English.

"What do you have in the way of a motor yacht charter?" Stone asked.

"Of motor yachts, we have only three," she said. "One is the Sultan of Saud's yacht, but that is nearing completion of a refit in a local yard and not ready for sailing yet. Then we have a thirty-foot Italian boat and a sixty-five-foot boat built in Germany."

"Have you photographs of them?"

She pointed at the wall behind her desk. "There," she said. "Let me get the files." She rummaged in a drawer and came up with two file folders.

Stone glanced at the thirty-footer, then moved on to the sixty-five-footer.

"It's pretty," Brio said.

"How long a charter?" the woman asked.

"A few days, no more than a week. We'd like to leave the yacht in Cairo."

She handed him a written description and more photos. "She's based in Alexandria. Would that be convenient? She's lying here now."

"Perhaps." Stone scanned the description. A crew of four, including a cook.

"She had a thorough refit last year and has been used only twice this year."

There was a discussion about money. She offered a better deal for cash, in dollars.

"Done," Stone said. "I'll get you the cash."

He and Brio walked out of the office and went to the car. Stone got a fistful of dollars from his valise.

"We're really going for a cruise?" Brio asked.

"It's a good way to search the coast. Have you got a better idea?"

"Nope."

They went back to the office, concluded the deal, and signed the contract. The woman called the yacht's captain, conversed, and hung up. "She can be ready to sail in an hour."

"Good," Stone said.

As they left, Stone turned to Brio. "Tell your agents in the Jeeps about our yacht, and to keep pace with us and look for signs of Zanian ashore."

Brio did so, and everybody got into the Jeeps. Half an hour later they saw the marina and their charter moored there.

Stone parked. "Tell your people to take our Jeep and meet us in Alexandria."

"Right."

Stone went aboard, found the captain, and asked him to send people to the car for their luggage.

Stone's phone rang. "Yes?"

"It's Faith. Zanian isn't here."

"All right, make for Cairo, same place we landed last time. Find a good hotel and get some rest. We'll be three or four days, coming by sea."

"As you wish."

Shortly, they were on board and drinking coffee while their luggage was stored.

49

Stone ordered dinner served on deck at seven o'clock, then went below, picked out a cabin for Wilcox, and put Brio in the one adjoining his and sharing a bath. His trunk was lying on a single berth in the master's cabin, next to a double. He put his valise next to it and tested the locks on both, then he stripped naked and got into the bigger berth. He was asleep almost at once.

He awoke and his wristwatch read five-thirty. Brio was asleep next to him. He got softly out of bed, went into the bath, and showered and shaved. Feeling refreshed he went back into his cabin and found Brio stretching and yawning. He tossed his robe aside and got into bed with her. "What you need," he said, "is some stimulation to bring you to full consciousness." He stimulated her, and she came to.

"I was afraid you wouldn't do that," she said after they had finished. "That's why I put myself in your way."

"You were a welcome impediment," he replied. "We'll do it again later, but right now we should dress for dinner."

"Black tie?" she asked. "A girl needs to know what to wear."

"I think just casual," he said. "I don't know if I have enough strength left to tie a necktie."

They had cocktails, and the captain came aft to speak to them. "Have you thought about an itinerary?" he asked.

"We'll want to sail at eight tomorrow morning and travel north, slowly, keeping near the eastern shore," Stone said. "We're looking for a friend." As he spoke, he looked out to see a very large yacht passing them, going south. "What on earth is that?"

"That is *Star of Saud*, the sultan's yacht. She has been in a yard for a refit for several months and must be out for sea trials now."

"She must be two hundred and fifty feet," Stone said.

"More like three hundred," the captain replied.

"I hope we'll get a better look at her," Stone said.

"I'll try and arrange that, if she's out tomorrow," the captain replied.

Dinner was served on the fantail, and Stone was once again relieved that it was lamb and humpless.

"I was aboard *Star* before her refit," Wilcox said. "She was sumptuous but looking worn. I expect she'll be like new after her relaunch. The sultan likes his possessions well-kept."

"We should have chartered her," Stone said, "since the FBI is paying."

"The director wouldn't like explaining that to a congressional committee," Brio said.

"Did you see a man on the afterdeck, smoking a cigar?" Wilcox asked.

"No," Stone replied.

"It could have been Zanian," he said, "though I wouldn't swear to it. He smokes Cuban cigars."

"If it were Zanian," Stone said, "it would be interesting to know how he made it from the sultan's dungeon to the sultan's yacht."

They all laughed.

Stone and Brio gave each other an encore at bedtime, and they slept well again.

Stone was awakened by the starting of engines and hit Brio on the backside to get her started.

By the time breakfast was served on deck they had left the marina and started north, Stone reckoned at about six knots: perfect. When they had finished breakfast, the captain brought binoculars for them. "To look for your friend," he said. "How is he traveling?"

"We've been out of touch," Stone said, "so I don't know." He raised the binoculars and examined the shoreline. They were leaving

Jeddah and there had been nothing ashore to attract Stone's notice. Now they were passing dozens of dhows, with their sails set for fishing. It was as he had imagined the Nile would have looked in earlier days.

"Lovely," Wilcox said, "if one is a romantic."

"One is," Stone replied.

They used the binoculars while Brio enjoyed the soft breeze over the deck. Shortly before lunchtime, the captain came aft and handed Stone a newspaper. "I'm sorry, I forgot to give you this at breakfast. It's the *International New York Times* from yesterday."

A small note among an array across the bottom of the front page caught Stone's eye:

There are rumors from Arabia that the sultan of Saud has put down a rebellion in his Sultanate.

Stone showed it to the others.

Wilcox spoke up, "I wouldn't put too much stock in the rumors," he said. "The sultan has to do this every few years, some say, just to show he is still in charge."

Stone wondered if it were true, and if it were, what, if anything, it would mean to their search for Zanian.

He watched the shoreline until dusk, then put away the binoculars.

50

After lunch the following day, while they were on coffee, a handsome runabout came alongside and offered an envelope, extended on a pole. Stone took it and found his name written in a florid style on the front. He opened it and found an invitation to dinner for the three of them that evening aboard *Star of Saud* at seven PM, black tie.

Stone looked at the boatman who shouted, "Yes? No?"

Stone nodded. "Yes!" he shouted back.

The man saluted him and drove away. Stone looked around: the big yacht was nowhere in sight.

"What was that about?" Brio asked.

"We've been invited to dinner aboard the royal yacht, *Star of Saud*," Stone said, handing her the envelope.

"Did we accept?"

"I decided for all of us: yes. I want to get a look at her, up close."

"Where is she?" Wilcox asked, looking around.

"A location wasn't specified, but they knew where to find us," Stone said. "I expect she'll turn up."

They were anchored in what passed for a cove, a mere indentation in the shoreline, when *Star* appeared at around five o'clock and with a great clatter of machinery and chain, dropped anchor a hundred yards away. Music—Vivaldi, Stone thought—wafted faintly across the water. The captain lowered the teak boarding steps for later use.

Everyone came on deck, dressed for dinner, at six-thirty, and at just before seven, the runabout they had seen earlier was lowered from an upper deck and motored over to their yacht. The captain of their yacht handed Stone a slip of paper. "This is my cell number. Call me if you need a ride back." The crew assisted them with boarding the tender, then they motored back to *Star*, which had larger and more accommodating boarding steps.

A white-jacketed crew member met them on the deck and invited them to follow him to the afterdeck for cocktails, and they did so.

A single man sat on the afterdeck, looking out to sea. He rose to greet them. He wore a naval-style dress uniform, or mess kit, trimmed with gold braid. It took Stone a moment to recognize

Colonel Said. Hands were shaken all round, they sat down, and a steward took drink orders.

"Colonel," Stone said, "I had not expected to see you at sea. Are you taking a vacation?"

"I am no longer a colonel," Said said. "I had thought you would have heard."

"Have you fallen out of favor with the sultan?" Wilcox asked.

"The sultan is now a prisoner in his own dungeon," Said said. "I am commanding general of all of Saud's armed forces."

Everyone was stunned into silence for a moment. Finally, Stone managed to speak, "I had not noticed the five-star insignia," he said. "We saw a mention in the *International New York Times* of rumors that the sultan had put down a rebellion."

"Hardly," Said said. "It was a bloodless coup."

"Well," Wilcox said, "I suppose congratulations are in order."

"Thank you."

Wilcox raised his glass. "The commanding general," he said, and they all drank. "In what condition is the sultan?" Wilcox asked.

"The sultan is unhappy."

"What are your intentions toward him?" Wilcox asked. "I ask these questions in my official capacity."

"He will receive a trial," Said said.

"What will be the charges?"

"I have left that in the hands of the judiciary. That is why I am here, to avoid even the appearance of influencing the court."

"Will the trial be public?"

"That, also, is in the hands of the court."

"If I may say so, while a public trial would be admirable in the eyes of the world, it would give the sultan an opportunity to both defend himself and to make accusations. It could be disruptive."

"The capital and the people are serene, as are the military. We have nothing to fear from the sultan's words. And while he has many wives and sons, he has never named a successor. His eldest son, an obvious candidate, has declared his personal loyalty to me, and has said that he has no wish to rule."

"Then," Stone said, "why are you here?"

"A little vacation, as you said. Others are working to smooth my path back. And after a few days or, perhaps, weeks, I shall return to Saud and take up my new position."

Wilcox spoke up again, "Have the Saudi Arabians expressed any view on the subject of the coup?"

"Their position is hands-off, and they have been hospitable to me. That said, no one but the king and you three know where I am. The relaunch of the yacht after her refitting came at an opportune moment."

"She is quite beautiful," Stone said.

"There is still a little work to be done on her. When everything is in order, I shall see that you all have the first tour."

"That would be very kind of you," Stone replied.

There was a brief silence, then Said spoke again, "I expect there is something you might wish to ask me," he said, with a slightly playful tone.

"May I?" Stone asked.

"Certainly, Mr. Barrington."

"General, where is Viktor Zanian?"

S aid smiled broadly. "By this point, Mr. Zanian is, no doubt, playing chess with the sultan," he replied.

"And what will be your disposition of him?"

"That remains to be seen."

Brio reached into her handbag and withdrew an envelope. "Copies of our arrest warrant and application for extradition are enclosed," she said. "Perhaps they might be of use to you."

Said accepted them and handed them to an aide. "Perhaps so, at the proper moment."

Wilcox spoke up, "How will you know when you have reached the 'proper moment'?"

"Forgive me for sounding venal, but Mr. Zanian has said that he will offer a billion dollars for his release, along with citizenship, a diplomatic passport, and appointment as the sultan's chief economic adviser."

"Then," Stone said, "why hasn't he come up with the billion dollars?"

"He has constantly expressed a willingness to do so, but complications have arisen."

"I'm not surprised," Stone said drily. "What are the complications?"

"The Treasury of the United States has issued a worldwide statement to financial institutions that, should any bank release funds at Mr. Zanian's request, to any other financial institution, person, or corporation, severe penalties will follow."

"Bless their little hearts," Brio muttered.

Said continued, "No financial institution wishes to be on the U.S. Treasury's . . . What do you call it?"

"Shit list," Stone replied.

"Ah, yes. Quite. Shit list."

"Perfectly understandable," Wilcox said.

"Mr. Zanian has given us to understand that he has at his immediate disposal a million and a quarter dollars in U.S. currency. While nothing like a billion, this is not as you say, food for chickens."

"Chicken feed," Stone said, helpfully.

"Quite so."

"Actually," Stone said, "Zanian does not have such a sum at his disposal. I, on the other hand, do."

"Are you telling me that you are willing to produce such a sum for Zanian?"

"I am telling you that should Viktor Zanian appear before me clean, well-fed, and in shackles, I would be willing to produce such a sum on receipt of an extradition order bearing your signature and seal. Or you can wait an eon or so for the United States Treasury to rescind its order."

"Then perhaps we can do business, Mr. Barrington."

"Perhaps we can, as long as it is understood that the sum in question represents the limit of my participation in such an arrangement."

"You make yourself very plain, sir."

"How shall we proceed?"

"I must make a few phone calls in pursuit of our deal, but everything is closed for business at this hour."

"Of course."

"I shall make these calls tomorrow morning, then be in touch."

"That is satisfactory. Perhaps at that time you could name a time and place for the delivery of Mr. Zanian's person."

"It would have to be at a venue outside the kingdoms of Saud and Saudi Arabia."

"May I suggest at Cairo International Airport, aboard my airplane?"

"You may, at a date and time to be set later."

"Not too much later, if you please."

"Quite. And now, perhaps we should indulge in your quaint Western custom of dinner?"

"As long as it doesn't involve the participation of a camel," Stone replied, smiling.

"I shall remark upon that to our chef." He rose and led them to a beautifully set table.

Two large, thick, and perfectly cooked porterhouse steaks were presented, carved, and served, except that the general was given a rack of lamb. All were given baked potatoes and haricots verts.

"The wines are Syrian," the general said.

They were deep, dark, and delicious.

Said found it necessary to speak on the telephone a couple of times during dinner, but otherwise, the evening went smoothly, until they were preparing to board the tender for the trip back to their yacht.

"There is one other thing that is important to our transfer of Mr. Zanian," the general said.

"I'm afraid, General," Stone said, "that in our previous discussion we set my limits for negotiation, and those I cannot exceed."

"Please be calm, Mr. Barrington," the general replied. "This is actually a matter between governments, or rather, between Ambassador Wilcox and me."

Stone shrugged.

"How may I be of help?" Wilcox asked.

"I wish that the legal department at your embassy will prepare a document for your signature that will remove any possibility of your government taking any steps for the recovery of Mr. Zanian's Gulfstream jet from the custody of the Sultanate, either in Saud or in any other country of the world, and acknowledging that the aircraft is now the property of the Sultanate."

"Ah, well," Wilcox said. "I can foresee two impediments to such an agreement."

"And what are these 'impediments'?" Said asked.

"First, any lien on the aircraft held by any financial institution anywhere, to secure, say, a loan, will have to be paid by the Sultanate in advance of the transaction."

"That is acceptable," Said said. "What else?"

"The aircraft is owned by Woodchip Corporation now. Because such a transaction involves the transfer of the aircraft from the ownership of an American corporation to a foreign entity, I am of insufficient rank to sign such a document on behalf of the United States. The signature of our secretary of state will be required. Or, of course, our president."

"Is it possible for you to obtain one of these signatures quickly?"

"I can but try," Wilcox said, "but I cannot guarantee the outcome."

"Then speak to whomever you must and give me an answer tomorrow."

"Of course," Wilcox said, and they shook hands. "Until tomorrow."

The party got into the tender, and it started home.

"He was obviously ready with that request earlier in the evening," Stone said.

"Yes, but he raised the subject at exactly the right moment," Wilcox replied.

"And you were ready with exactly the right answer," Stone said.

"I was, in my youth," Wilcox said, "an attorney-at-law."

52

Stone, Brio, and Wilcox sat on the fantail of their chartered yacht, while Wilcox typed out the document Said had demanded.

"There," Wilcox said, turning around the laptop and handing it to Stone. "Do you wish to add or subtract anything?" he asked.

Stone read it through. "I think it's perfect, and that it would be dangerous to change anything."

Wilcox removed his State Department cell phone from a jacket pocket and speed-dialed a number, while pacing around the deck, conducting a conversation with someone. Finally, he hung up. "The secretary of state is on Air Force 3, having departed for Tokyo half an hour ago. The telephone and e-mail electronics aboard the aircraft are inoperable, so he will be out of touch until the airplane lands at Tokyo and he is able to travel to our embassy there. We're talking seventeen, eighteen hours."

"That leaves the president," Stone said.

"It does. Ordinarily, she does not accept telephone calls from State Department personnel of my rank, except in the direst circumstances, like the bombing of an embassy, and in the absence of the secretary of state. I am not inclined to attempt to breach that barrier under these circumstances."

"I see," Stone said, knowing what was coming next.

"It is my understanding that you and the president are . . . rather, have . . . a close personal relationship. Is that so?"

Stone thought about it for a moment. "I have heard that rumor, too."

"Do you think that, given the circumstances, you might communicate this letter to her directly, and ask her to sign and transmit it to both me and the secretary of state."

Stone thought some more. "You are aware, are you not, that I have a financial interest in the successful completion of this transaction?"

Wilcox winced and sucked his teeth for a moment. "I am very much afraid that I neglected to incorporate that fact into my calculations. My apologies."

"No apology necessary, Henry," Stone said.

Everyone quietly sipped his cognac for a while. Then Brio spoke up, "I have been in the presence of the director of the FBI on occasions when he communicated directly with the president on Bureau business. Perhaps I can call him and ask him to call her."

"What a good idea," Wilcox said.

"Perhaps," Stone said, pensively. "However . . ."

After a long pause, Brio said, "However what?"

"Brio," Stone said, "the ten-million-dollar reward for Zanian is being offered by the FBI, isn't it?"

"Yes."

"What is the source of those funds?"

"I was wrong. The money would come from something called FBI Emeritus, which is an organization made up of retired, high-ranking Bureau officials."

"This is a private, nongovernmental organization?"

"Yes. It's all very quiet. Most people at the Bureau have never heard of it."

"Question: Where would an association of former government officials get their hands on ten million dollars?"

A dead silence ensued, for a count of about twenty.

"I don't know," Brio said, finally.

"Is the director currently a member of this group?"

"Yes, members are usually elected upon the achievement of the rank of assistant director, at a minimum."

"Stone," Wilcox said, "are you leery of accepting the reward, given its origins?"

"Certainly not!" Stone snorted. "I'll take their money in the blink of an eye!"

"Then, what . . ."

"I'm leery of establishing even the slightest connection of the president with a private club, which has ready access to that kind of money. Where did they get it? What other 'projects' have they funded? Secret wars? Black operations? Assassinations of foreign dignitaries? The trail could lead anywhere."

"But you don't mind it leading to you," Wilcox said.

"If a connection arose, I could deny all knowledge of the source of the funds. I could claim, as anyone else could, that I have no idea of the money's origin—and I can do it without igniting an investigation by a congressional committee. The president, on the other hand, has political enemies who would enjoy nothing better than hauling her into a committee room, putting her under oath, and eventually, shipping her off to Guantánamo for a little vacation."

"So to speak," said Wilcox.

"Well, yes," Stone said, "but you get the point."

"I do."

"Sorry," Brio said. "Bad idea."

"We all have them," Stone said. "I think it would be better if the secretary of state called the president, or better yet, just signed off on it himself. After all, the only purpose of the document is to keep the United States from getting its hands on an airplane that the sultan—or rather, Said, the commanding general of the armed forces, has the hots for."

"Well put," Wilcox said. "The entire staff of the State Department couldn't have said it better."

Brio spoke up, "Henry, I don't suppose you could just sort of give Said your word that you won't go after the Gulfstream?"

Wilcox burst out laughing. "My dear, in the circumstances that Said is considering, my word is nothing more than a puff of hot air."

"Let's sleep on this," Stone said, rising.

"Always a good idea," Wilcox said, rising, too.

They went off to bed.

53

Stone and Brio were at breakfast the following morning when Henry Wilcox joined them, later than usual.

"Oversleep, Henry?" Stone asked.

"No, I got up early this morning and sent the document for the secretary's signature, plus an explanation of the circumstances, to his personal e-mail address, so that as soon as he is in a location with access to electronics, he will find them waiting for him."

"Assuming he checks his e-mail," Stone said. "We all fail to do that, sometimes."

"He's pretty good about it," Wilcox replied. "At least, we can tell Said that we've sent it to him and are awaiting a reply."

"Good point. We can tell him that we've done all we can, and that the secretary's response time is out of our hands."

"I don't expect he'll find that comforting," Wilcox said, "but he should find it plausible."

"Let's hope so. Said said last night that Zanian had offered a billion dollars, but he didn't say how much Zanian had been able to raise so far."

"And that is a bit of information I'd like to have," Wilcox said.

"I take it as a good sign that Said is still interested in our two million and a quarter dollars," Stone said.

"He's not going to pass that up for a billion-dollar pipe dream of Zanian's," Brio said.

"Let's hope not."

The yacht's captain came aft. "Mr. Barrington, a call for you on the ship's radiotelephone." He handed Stone a portable handset. "Just press the button marked 'answer.'"

Stone accepted the phone and put it on the table. "This is odd," he said. "A radiotelephone call can be heard by anyone with a radio tuned to the correct frequency."

"You'd better answer," Brio said.

Stone pressed the answer button. "Yes?"

"Am I speaking to whom I think I am?" It was a voice that sounded like Said.

"That depends on whom you think I am."

"When did we last dine?"

"Last evening."

"What was missing from your dinner?"

Stone thought about that for a moment. "A hump," he said, finally.

"Has the document of which we spoke last evening been completed?"

"Yes, and sent to the mailbox of the intended addressee," Stone replied. "He is presently in a distant location and electronically unavailable, until some services can be restored."

"In what time frame?"

"We are unable to divine that from our present position."

Said made an angry noise.

"You understand this is quite out of our hands?"

"I suppose."

"May I return this call when we know more?"

"Yes, but use the cell number."

"Roger. Out." Stone ended the call. "He is unhappy."

Wilcox shrugged. "So am I."

"I still don't understand why he used the radiotelephone."

"Perhaps his own electronic services are temporarily unavailable."

"Good. If so, he understands our problem. Do you think it's worth trying to reach the secretary again?"

"I can try," Wilcox said, taking out his phone and pressing a single digit. He listened for a moment. "This time I got a recorded message, saying the service I seek is temporarily unavailable."

"That is not an improvement on the situation," Brio said.

"No, it isn't," Wilcox said. "It appears that we are going to have to exercise the most difficult skill of diplomacy."

"And what is that?" Brio asked.

"Patience," Wilcox replied.

"Well, shit!" Brio responded.

"Perhaps so, but it is all I have to offer."

"Relax, Henry," Stone said. "Nobody's blaming you, not even Said."

"Thank you."

"My own personal motto is *Si non nunc quando*," Stone said.

Wilcox laughed, something he did not do often.

Brio looked puzzled. "What is that, pig Latin?"

"Just plain Latin," Wilcox said. "As anyone with a New England schoolboy's prep-school education can tell you, it means: 'If not now, when?'"

"Well translated."

"Where did you prep, Stone?"

"At P.S. Six, in New York City."

Wilcox laughed uproariously. His cell phone rang. "Yes? Good morning, General. Is your cell service working again?"

"It is, as you can see."

"So is that of the secretary of state," Wilcox lied.

"And what is the disposition?"

"He has approved the language of the document and is transmitting a signed copy to me."

"When?"

"As soon as their service is fully operational. It shouldn't be later than this afternoon."

"I shall look forward to receiving it."

"If you will give me a secure e-mail address, I will forward it to you as soon as I receive it." He made a note of the address. "I shall speak to you later," Wilcox said, then hung up.

"Excuse me, Henry, but that was a lie."

"I am aware of that, Stone. Lying is sometimes just another tool in the diplomatic toolbox."

"And what tool in your toolbox will you use to obtain the secretary's signature on the document?"

"An equally good one," Wilcox said. "Forgery."

54

Wilcox pressed send, then waited. Presently, the captain came aft with two pages from his printer and handed them to the diplomat.

"Do they meet your standards?" Stone inquired.

"Not yet, but soon." He took a Mont Blanc fountain pen from an inside pocket and scrawled something on a blank sheet of paper, then repeated the process. "Now," he said. He took the two copies of the document and fluently signed them both, then inspected his work. "Excellent, if I may say so," he said, handing them to Stone.

"I've no idea what the signature of the secretary of state looks like," he said.

"That's all right," Wilcox replied. "Neither does General Said. It's close enough to fool anybody but, perhaps, the secretary's own secretary."

Stone found an envelope, folded a sheet, and tucked it inside, sealing it with a lick. He picked up his cell phone and dialed a number. "General?"

"Yes?"

"This is Stone Barrington. We have received the expected communication from the secretary of state. We have sent you an electronic copy. How would you like the document delivered?"

"I'll send the boatman, with his clever stick."

"When?"

"Immediately."

"Will you call me back when you have seen the document?"

"Of course." He hung up.

Across the water Stone could see a figure jump into *Star's* tender and head his way. Stone watched as he approached, then stepped up to the rail. The boatman thrust his stick upward, and Stone grabbed it, thrust the envelope into the jaws of the clip at its end, and watched as the boatman brought it aboard, tucked it into his jacket pocket, and returned to the royal yacht. "Now," he said to Wilcox and Brio.

They watched as the boatman reached the yacht, secured the tender, ran up the boarding stairs, and disappeared. They went back to their comfortable seats on the fantail. A moment later Stone's cell phone rang. "Stone Barrington."

"Mr. Barrington, this is General Said."

"I rather thought that it might be."

"I have the document in my hand."

"And does it meet your requirements?"

"In every respect."

"I am pleased to hear it. Now, when do we receive the corpus delicti of Mr. Zanian?"

"We must first find and sober up his airplane's crew, then negotiate the plane's release from your Jeeps at the airport, then it can proceed to Cairo. Two or three days, I expect."

"I had hoped for a more immediate surrender."

"May I suggest that you and your party pack and move to *Star*? There is, of course, plenty of room, and you will be made very comfortable, then we can continue to Cairo in one yacht instead of two."

"What a good idea! We'll be ready for your boatman in an hour."

"Very good. Drinks at six-thirty, on the fantail. And please don't forget your trunk."

"That will be brought to Cairo on my aircraft, at the appointed time for the exchange with Mr. Zanian."

"Fair enough," Said said. "See you at six-thirty. We're dressing for dinner."

"Of course. Goodbye." They both hung up.

"We're moving to the royal yacht, which will convey us to Cairo," Stone said. "Go and pack. The boat will be here for us in an hour, and we may as well change for dinner now. It's black tie again."

"Oh, shoot!" Brio said. "Now I have to come up with another dress."

"Judging from the capacity of your luggage and the number of cases, that won't be a problem," Stone said.

S tone settled with the captain and crew, and they were efficiently conveyed to *Star* as soon as the boat arrived. As they sat on the fantail, awaiting the arrival of their host, the usual noises associated with getting under way could be heard. From somewhere far below the engines changed their whisper to a murmur, and the big yacht weighed anchor and proceeded up the Red Sea, in good order.

The general, in yet another naval uniform, made his appearance on the fantail, and his guests rose to meet him.

"What a fine evening it will be," he said, while being handed a large whiskey. "And I am so fortunate to have you all to share it with."

They settled into their comfortable chairs, and refills were served.

"General," Wilcox said, "is there a Mrs. Said?"

"Several," Said replied, blithely.

"Of course," Wilcox replied. "The joys of your faith and your high standing. Tell me, what becomes of the sultan's harem in these changing circumstances?"

"I suppose that rather depends on what becomes of the sultan," Said said.

Wilcox did not pursue that line of conversation further.

"What changes do you intend for your country, in your new regime?" Stone asked.

"Women will have equal standing, for the first time."

"Hurrah for women!" Brio shouted.

"And what else?" Wilcox asked.

"Little else," Said replied. "I have, as a practical matter, been running the country for some time. I expect a fairly seamless transition."

"My country hopes there will not be bloodshed," Wilcox said.

"We can both hope, Mr. Ambassador," Said replied. "However, there will always be those who insist on having their blood shed, won't there be? In those cases we will endeavor to be swift and sure, to cause as little pain as possible."

His three guests gulped simultaneously.

55

Stone was practically lifted out of his bed by the loudest noise he had ever heard. He jumped up and swept back the curtain on the portside porthole. A few yards away an enormous container ship was passing, headed south. It was its horn that had greeted Stone's new day. They were clearly in the Suez Canal, having steamed all night. He fell back into bed next to Brio, who was sitting up in bed, wide-eyed.

"Relax, it's only the largest ship you've ever seen, and you could hit it with a slingshot. It's nice to see you so awake, though," he said, pulling the sheet down and crawling into bed with her. He laid his head on her belly and worked his way south.

"Promise me we won't hear that noise again," she said, arranging herself to greet him.

"I can only promise you that this is going to feel very, very good," he said, attending to the business at hand.

She ran her fingers through his hair. "You're right," she said.

After Stone had proved his point a couple of times, he raised the issue of breakfast. "May I have it served on your belly?" he asked.

"No, it will either be too hot or too cold. Why don't you raise your attention to above my waist, and we'll discuss it?" He did so, and they discussed it, deciding to get up and have breakfast on deck.

Wilcox joined them shortly. "Did you hear that?"

"Hear what?" Stone asked. "I didn't hear anything."

"Nor did I," Brio said innocently.

It took another moment before they all collapsed, laughing.

"That was the loudest noise I've ever heard," Wilcox said.

"Us, too," Stone replied.

The landscape was desert on both sides of the canal. Occasionally vehicles passed on the roads on either side of them, headed in both directions. Other ships, large and small, passed.

"I've had breakfast on a canal before," Stone said, "but not one this big."

"Oh," Wilcox said, "I saw Said briefly on my way up, and he asked me to tell you that we will conduct the exchange for Zanian at Port Said Airport, tomorrow at midday, instead of Cairo, and to inform your air crew."

"I wonder how long the runway is at Port Said," Stone said.

"It's 7,700 feet. He told me that, too."

"We can manage that." He called Faith.

"Yes, sir?"

"Change of destination," he said. "Our meeting will be at Port Said tomorrow at midday, instead of Cairo. They've got a 7,700-foot runway."

"That's good. I'll have two agents aboard to deal with Mr. Zanian."

"Fine. And be sure that my large trunk and valise are in a position where they will be easy to unload."

"Got it. Will we go directly from Port Said to Teterboro?"

"Yes, if we've got the fuel for it."

"Barring extraordinary headwinds, we have, but we can always refuel at Santa Maria, in the Azores, if necessary. I'll get the forecast."

"Good. See you tomorrow." They hung up.

"I had a strange dream last night," Wilcox said.

"Oh?"

"I dreamed I was in a Dickens novel."

"Poor you. I hope you weren't Oliver Twist."

"No, I was Tiny Tim."

"Well, you've recovered. You don't look any tinier."

"I'm relieved to hear it."

Stone changed the subject, reflecting that there was hardly anything more boring that someone else's dreams.

General Said came up from below. "Good morning to you all," he said.

"I gave your message to Stone," Wilcox said.

"Stone, I hope the change is not inconvenient," Said said.

"On the contrary, it is quite convenient. From Port Said we can be off to America in the early afternoon, assuming everything goes smoothly. General, do you have any reason to suppose that things might not go as smoothly as we wish?"

"None whatever," Said replied.

"By the way, you said that Zanian was trying to raise money from his various accounts but not having much success?"

"That is correct."

"Exactly how much success is Ms. Zanian not having?"

Said smiled. "I'm told he has raised only a few million dollars."

"And where do those dollars now reside?"

"Apparently, in a bank account that Zanian still has access to."

"Just not one of his bigger accounts?"

"Quite."

"Was it the sultan's idea or yours to sell him his freedom for a billion dollars?"

"It was Zanian's idea," Said replied.

"And whose idea was it to accept that deal?"

"The sultan and I never had an affirmative agreement on that subject."

"Did the possible gaining of a billion dollars have anything to do with the, ah, change in the sultan's status?"

Said shrugged. "You might say that. Then again, you might say the opposite. I shall leave that for the historians to work out. Why do you ask?"

"Because I am wondering why you are content to accept my two million and a quarter, when there is at least the prospect of a billion."

"I regard that prospect as the dream of an opium eater," Said replied. "I prefer to deal in cash I can run my fingers through and which is acceptable at any financial institution."

"I perceive that you are not a dreamer, General, but rather a practical man."

"It is one of the differences the sultan and I have had over the years," Said replied. Then he concerned himself with ordering breakfast.

When he was done with the waiter, he asked Stone, "Tell me, what would you like for dinner this evening? Something else without a hump?"

"If you please."

"It is our last evening aboard this yacht. Is there something you would like to request?"

"Osso buco," Stone said. "A dish of veal shank."

"I'm sure the chef can come up with a shank, instead of a hump," Said said, laughing.

56

Stone sat on a chaise longue on the upper deck, a cool drink and Brio on one side of him. It was the first time he had seen her in a bikini, and it was a small one.

"I think we should have you photographed in that swimsuit," he said. "The result, pinned to a bulletin board in the Hoover building, would be a big hit, I'm sure."

She laughed. "Ordinarily I conceal my figure at work, even under clothing. I don't think anyone in the building knows that I have breasts."

"Perhaps I should spread the word," Stone said. "You'd become very popular."

"No one would believe you," she replied. "I've been that careful."

"Does your new rank permit a change in costume?"

"If I did that, the director would think he'd made a terrible mistake in promoting me. I think I'll let sleeping breasts lie."

Stone picked up a bottle of lotion and spread some on his face, then put on a straw hat. "Is there anything I can lubricate for you?" he asked, raising the bottle.

"Thank you, no. I'm quite well oiled."

"You smell like a coconut," he said. "It's very pleasant."

"I'm happy to be an olfactory success."

"Have you spoken to your squad of agents lately?"

"Yes, they'll meet us in Port Said."

"Apparently, Faith already has a couple of volunteers to sit on Zanian during the trip back."

"I wonder what she offered them," Brio said.

"Oh, Faith can be quite alluring, even in her uniform. Perhaps, *especially* in her uniform."

"In my experience, special agents respond favorably to allure. Are two men enough?"

"For Faith or for Zanian?"

Brio laughed. "For Zanian."

"Well, once we're off the ground, Zanian has nowhere to run, so even if they unshackle him for the toilet, he's not going to parachute out over Long Island before landing."

"I suppose not."

"Have you arranged a reception committee for Zanian?" Stone asked.

"Yes, our airplane, containing the other twenty-two agents, will precede us to Teterboro, and they will receive him. There'll be suitable transport waiting when we land."

Wilcox joined them, wearing a terry-cloth robe. He shucked it off, revealing a wiry and athletic physique, for a man of, what, sixty?

"Welcome, Henry," Stone said.

"Last chance for a bit of sun," Wilcox replied.

"What are your plans after Port Said?" Stone asked.

"May I hitch a ride to New York with you?" the ambassador asked. "I've got some leave coming."

"Of course. I'd be happy to have you as a guest at my house. You'll be almost as comfortable as on this yacht."

"I may take you up on that for a couple of days," Wilcox replied. "I'll have to go on to Washington, eventually, to make my report."

"As you wish. I'll have the housekeeper make up a room for you."

"You're very kind, Stone."

"What about you, Brio?" Stone asked. "I recall that you are homeless in New York."

"That will be up to my director," she said. "He may have some immediate reassignment for me. May I let you know on short notice?"

"Of course. Perhaps I'll have some people in for dinner."

"The Bacchettis, of course."

"At least, Dino. Viv's schedule is unpredictable."

"Have you any firearms aboard, Stone?" Wilcox asked, unexpectedly.

"I have a .380 pistol and permits from both the city and the CIA, allowing me to carry it pretty much wherever I like. Why do you ask? Do you think someone will need shooting?"

"It occurred to me that Zanian might need protecting," Wilcox said. "There are a great many angry people waiting for him."

"He'll be in FBI custody. I'll let them worry about it."

"I don't know why I'm asking," Wilcox said. "I wouldn't be upset, if someone put a few bullets into him."

"I hope you didn't invest with him," Stone said.

Wilcox laughed. "Diplomats don't have enough money to invest, unless they've inherited it. My family money is in a well-tended trust. What are you going to do with your reward money?"

"I owe half of it to my friend Dino Bacchetti, who was very helpful at the beginning of all this."

"The police commissioner?"

"One and the same. We were policemen together, once upon a time."

"And the other half?"

"I guess I'll reimburse myself."

"That seems fair. You must be out a lot in expenses, though."

"I have a contract with the FBI, covering most of my costs. I'll submit a bill in due course."

"I'll run interference on that," Brio said.

"Brio," Wilcox said, "how did you come by your Christian name?"

"The usual way, from my mother, who believed she was half Italian. Her mistake. That half turned out to be Polish."

"Oh, well."

"That's what my mother said when she learned the truth."

"Henry," Stone said, "will the State Department send you back to the Sultanate?"

"Probably not. I don't think that the overthrow of the sultan would merit an A-plus on my record. I've got only a couple of years before I can retire, so it could be anywhere they have an open slot."

"Surely they can't blame you for the change in regime," Stone said.

"They can blame me for not seeing it coming. If they want to."

"Is there anything I can do? Write a letter to somebody, or something?"

"Oh, I don't think so. That could actually make things worse. Let sleeping tigers lie."

"So be it."

"I bet you'll be the only diplomat who's spent any time with the sultan's replacement," Brio said.

"I suppose so. If I wanted to go back, I'd use that as a qualification. Maybe it's time for someplace green and pleasant, like England. I've always liked England."

"I have a friend in the foreign office," Stone said.

"The foreign minister?"

"No, she's head of MI6."

"Ah, the Secret Intelligence Service. I don't think Felicity would be much help in the circumstances."

Clouds began to appear in the sky, and it felt cooler on deck. The group adjourned to dress for their last dinner aboard *Star*.

Back in their cabin, Stone watched Brio shed her bikini, which
didn't take long, and they made love in a relaxed manner for a
while.

Finally, when they were resting, Stone said, "Any chance you'll
get an assignment in New York?"

"Maybe. If the AIC shoots himself before we get back. I think
it's more likely that the director will send me to Washington for
seasoning in the new job. *But*, if somebody retires, or screws up and
he has a need for an AD, then I could end up anywhere."

"In your heart of hearts, where would you want to be?"

"Maybe West Coast, San Francisco or even L.A."

"Not New York?"

She slapped him on the ass smartly. "I wouldn't mind."

"Are we going to have a lot of press to greet us at Teterboro?"

"Now, that's an interesting question. I haven't made a move in that direction, but the director could have, if he feels he needs some favorable PR, and who doesn't? I plan to deliver Zanian and then be ready for anything."

"I think you should be ready to become the most famous FBI assistant director in the Bureau," Stone said. "Unless your director makes a conscious effort to keep you out of it, the press will sniff you out for the details, and if you won't talk to them, they'll make it up."

"God, I hadn't thought about that."

"You'd better whip up a few quotable lines and take notes, then brace yourself. Staying at my house would be better than trying to hide in a hotel. All you need is a car with a driver who doesn't know where he's going until you tell him. You can send your bags to the house with me, then have your driver let you out a block away. There's a secret entrance to the garden behind my house. I can meet you there and make you disappear."

"Well, now, I haven't been thinking ahead, have I?"

"Perhaps not." He gave her directions to the garden entrance and a key. Then he took a shower and had a shave. Brio joined him for the shower, but after she'd scrubbed his back, he left her to it and went to get dressed.

The yacht's crew had pressed his tux and laundered his other things, even polished his shoes. He left his cabin, and someone was cleaning the staircase he normally used, so he walked farther aft toward another one. Then there was that noise. Instantly, he thought of Wilcox's Dickensian dream and realized that the sound in his dream had been the dragging of chains.

Stone froze and listened. All quiet for a moment. He came to a big watertight door, then stopped and put his ear to it. Nothing. He thought about spinning the big wheel on the door and going even farther aft, but Said might not view such actions as those of a gentlemanly guest. So he took the stairs and emerged on deck. He found Wilcox already enjoying his first drink.

"Henry," Stone said, joining him. "Do you know . . ."

But a crew member appeared, took his drink order, and poured it. When they were alone again, Stone said, "Henry, I've been thinking about your dream."

"My Tiny Tim dream?"

"Yes."

"What about it?"

"Did you hear a noise in your dream? Something like chains being dragged?"

Wilcox sat up. "Yes, I did."

"In your travels around this yacht, have you encountered anything that looked like a brig?"

"'A brig'?"

"Like a jail cell on a naval vessel."

"No, but I don't know what's aft of that watertight door near my cabin. What are you thinking?"

"That there may be someone imprisoned on the yacht."

"Well, that would be right in line with the sultan's view on dungeons. An unruly crew member, perhaps?"

"Perhaps. I was thinking Viktor Zanian."

"But why?"

"Maybe he bought a ticket, paid for with some of his ill-gotten gains."

"A ticket to Port Said?"

"Originally to Cairo, now the destination has changed."

"Why would he want that?"

"To get him out of the Sultanate before somebody decides to let the sultan out of his dungeon?"

Wilcox shook his head. "I don't see that."

"If he managed to free up some millions of his stash in the world's banks it might interest Said enough for him to get Zanian out of the Sultanate. I mean, the commanding general is mighty interested in my two million and a quarter. Zanian has a lot more than that, and it might be enough to interest Said, if his prisoner can get his hands on some of it."

"That's a rational view, I think."

"Zanian is a wily enough character to have some of the money he stole stashed someplace where the government can't get their hands on it. All he would need is his freedom and a computer."

"And a little help from Said," Wilcox said, thoughtfully.

58

Stone raised his glass to Brio and Wilcox. "Smooth sailing," he said.

"That sounds like you're not expecting it," Brio said.

"I'm uncertain. It's just a feeling. Listen. Do you think you could spare a couple more special agents to fly to Teterboro with us?"

"You don't think two are enough?" Wilcox asked.

"I'd like some backup," Stone said.

Brio looked at her watch. "Well, you're a little late. Their airplane landed in Port Said yesterday, and everybody was checked into a hotel for some rest and showers and a change to civilian clothes. They took off this morning for Teterboro."

Stone sighed. "Well, I took too long to make that judgment," he said.

"Zanian is a pudgy little guy," Brio said. "Why do you think that two burly FBI agents can't handle him?"

"I know, I know. I'm just a belt-and-suspenders guy, I guess."

"I've never noticed that about you before," she said.

"Forget it. It's out of the question now."

"I can help them out, if necessary," Wilcox said. "I was once a security guard at the State Department, during my university days."

"And I'll bet you were a tough guy," Brio said.

"Tough enough for the job. I tossed a few people out of the building, and all of them were bigger than I. Zanian isn't."

"Thanks for the thought, Henry," Stone said. "I guess we can both pitch in if the going gets rough."

The commanding general made his entrance and was handed a martini. "Our last evening," he said, raising his glass.

Everybody drank.

"General," Stone said. "Does this yacht have a brig?"

"'A brig'?"

"A naval term for a jail cell."

"Yes, of course," Said said. "That is a normal element of our security aboard. One never knows what one may encounter."

"Is there anyone incarcerated at the moment?"

"Yes, a sailor who made unwanted advances on one of the chef's assistants. She's a lovely young woman. The man seemed unable to contain himself, so we locked him up. He'll be dealt with on arrival in Port Said."

"How will he be dealt with?"

"The captain will determine that. I've no interest in the matter. Why do you ask about this?"

"We thought we heard ghostly chains rattling."

"Then perhaps you did, Stone. You're not crazy after all, eh?"

"I'm relieved to learn that," Stone said.

"What is it Occam's razor says?"

"If you hear the sound of hoofbeats, think horses, not zebras."

"Quite. And when you hear chains rattling, think prisoner, not ghost."

"Good advice."

"And what are your plans after tomorrow, Stone?"

"As soon as we've secured Mr. Zanian aboard, we'll take off for Teterboro. I expect to sleep in my own bed tomorrow night."

"Not alone, I hope," Said said, chuckling.

"That remains to be seen," Stone replied.

"And, Brio, what are your plans?"

"That will be up to the director of the FBI," she said.

"Wilcox?"

"I'll need to report to the State Department in Washington and, while I'm at it, see if I have a new assignment."

"I hope we will continue to have you in the Sultanate. Would you like me to make an official request?"

"Perhaps it would be better for you to have someone who is more trainable. I'm pretty set in my ways."

"We would be delighted to have you stay on, but whatever you and the State Department want is fine with us."

"One thing they will want to know about in Washington," Wilcox said, "is the disposition of the sultan."

"It's not entirely up to me, so you will have to wait until I've had time to consult with my administration."

"Then we will be patient."

"What is it they say: 'Patience will be rewarded'?"

"That is axiomatic, but sometimes we don't like the reward," Wilcox replied.

They were called to dinner.

Later, as they were undressing for bed, Brio began rubbing Stone's shoulders and neck. He moved so as to give her better access.

"What's worrying you, Stone?" she asked. "I've never seen you worried before."

"I'm not worried, exactly. It's just that I don't like being in a position where I can't control what's happening."

"I never thought you were a control freak," she said.

"I've never thought of myself as that, either, but maybe I have a touch of the condition. Once we've concluded our business, I want to leave immediately, no delays."

"Perfectly okay with me, but delays do occur at airports, and I don't think that Egyptian ones are an exception to that. You need to just relax."

"What you're doing right now is good for what ails me," Stone said.

"Take off your trousers and stretch out on the bed. I'll do even better things."

He did, and she did.

They woke up the following morning without motion or engine noises. Stone looked out a window. The sun was rising, and they were moored in a marina containing all sorts of craft, none of them the size of *Star*.

Stone dressed quietly, so as not to waken Brio, then went on deck and looked around. People, mostly professional crews, were stirring on other craft, hosing down decks, boarding provisions, and sending garbage bags ashore.

Stone walked to the afterdeck, and a crew member appeared and asked if he required breakfast and if so, what? Stone had just ordered scrambled eggs and sausages when Henry Wilcox appeared on deck and put in his own order. They were brought a thermos of coffee and sat down.

"How are you this morning, Stone?" Wilcox asked.

"A little nervous," Stone replied. "I just want to get this done and get out of here."

Stone's phone rang and he answered.

"It's Faith," she said. "We'll be serviced and ready to taxi at ten AM."

"I'll arrange for the boarding of your passenger about that time, perhaps a little earlier, if I can manage it."

"Your two FBI special agents are boarding as we speak," she said.

"Send everybody out for breakfast and have them back in an hour," Stone replied. "I'll be in touch."

"All is well, I presume," Wilcox said.

"All is as well as can be expected," Stone said. Breakfast arrived, and they tucked into it. Brio arrived shortly and settled for pastries and coffee.

"Where is your airplane?" she asked.

"At the airport. So are your two agents."

"That was my information. I think they're ready for anything. Where is the exchange going to take place?"

"At the airplane. That's where the money is, so if Said wants it, that's where he'll have to go."

"I hope you're more relaxed than you were last night," she said, placing a cool hand on his cheek.

"Thanks to your ministrations, yes."

"Anytime."

"Henry, have you had any communication from the secretary of state?"

"Yes, and with approval of our arrangement."

"So, you're no longer a forger."

"Pure as the driven snow."

Their host, in a khaki uniform, but with his new rank displayed, appeared, greeted them one by one, and joined them, looking cheerful. "I trust you all slept well," he said. "And if you are packed, the crew will see to your luggage soon. Are you all going to the airport?"

"Yes, we're all traveling on the same aircraft, General."

"Ambassador Wilcox, too?"

"I'm thumbing a ride," Wilcox said, making hitchhiking motions.

"Ah, yes, an American expression. I saw it in an excellent film with Clark Gable."

"And Claudette Colbert," Brio said. *It Happened One Night.*"

"Quite so, and it did," Said replied. His breakfast appeared before him, and he attended to it.

"And so, Stone," Said said, sipping his coffee. "You wish to make the exchange at your airplane?"

"That is correct. Where is Mr. Zanian?"

"He is arriving shortly, aboard his own airplane—his own until he departs in yours. The documents are all in order." He reached into a pocket and detached a small key from a clump of others. "This is the key to Mr. Zanian's shackles," he said.

Stone slipped it into his pocket. "Thank you."

"And where is your money?"

"It will appear, as if by magic, at the airplane. Shall we say, nine o'clock?"

"That will do nicely."

Stone took a checkbook from his jacket pocket. "I'm afraid I dipped into the valise for the charter fee of our yacht," he said. "I hope my check for that sum will be acceptable."

"Oh, please," the general said, waving a hand. "Let us not quibble over small sums. Your charter is on me."

"I would like to keep my valise," Stone said, "since it is part of a matched set of luggage. Perhaps you could bring along something to put that part of the cash in."

"Of course. I would not wish to spoil a matched set."

Stone looked at his watch. "Well, we have nothing to do until we leave for the airport. What time will that be?"

"It's not far; say, eight-thirty?"

"Excellent. Brio, are you packed?"

"Yes, my bags are on our berth, with yours."

"Henry?"

"All ready for pick up," Wilcox responded. Then he turned to Said. "General, perhaps you could satisfy my curiosity on your intentions toward the sultan. The secretary is concerned. He asked me about it in our conversation yesterday."

The general leaned back in his chair. "I can give you only my current thinking," he said. "Things could change, if he proves to be as obstreperous as he usually is."

"Please," Wilcox said.

"There is a small oasis, somewhere in the Arabian Desert, perhaps two or three hundred miles from anywhere, and a comfortable residence is being made ready for him there. He will be provided with everything he desires, except transportation—not so much as a camel."

"Does his son approve?"

"His son would be harsher, if he were acting alone. He will

continue to be schooled by me in the arts of governing, with an occasional lecture on compassion."

"Always attractive in a ruler."

"When he is ready, I will retire."

"To where?"

"I have a number of places in mind, one or two of them in the United States. I hope I may have your kind help in dealing with the State Department."

"Of course, assuming they have not yet put me out to pasture."

"They are far too wise for that," the general said, standing. "Ah well, I have some phone calls to make. A large Mercedes van will call for us in time for an eight-thirty departure."

They stood and saw him off, then sat again.

Wilcox poured them more coffee. "Still nervous, Stone?"

"Yes," Stone replied. "Perhaps more than ever."

60

Their transportation arrived, and Stone watched the yacht's crew load the luggage into a rear compartment. Said appeared by the van and beckoned to them.

The van was quite luxurious inside, much like a private jet, Stone reflected. There were four seats in the rear, two facing two. They took seats as instructed by Said, and Stone found himself facing the rear, directly opposite the general.

"Are you comfortable?" Said asked him.

"Of course," Stone replied, uncomfortably. He did not like not being able to see where they were going. The driver and another man climbed into the driver's and front passenger's seats. The van started and moved away from the yacht.

"Goodbye, *Star*," Brio said as they moved away from the dock. "General, what a wonderful yacht!" she said. "Thank you so much for having us aboard."

"It was my great pleasure," Said replied. "It would be fun to cruise in the Med sometime, perhaps the Greek Islands?"

"*Star* is her own island," Brio said.

Stone watched the marina disappear as they drove away. He had a view of the canal, looking out and aft, and a tanker was headed south.

"Extraordinary feat of engineering, isn't it?" Said asked.

"'Extraordinary' is the right word," Stone said. He suddenly found that he missed his pistol, which was in his briefcase with its holster and silencer, and the case was in the rear of the van with the luggage. Why had Wilcox asked him if he were armed? Was he expecting something Stone had missed?

After half an hour or so, they made a turn and slowed. Apparently, gates were being opened for them. The van made a left turn, then a 180 turn, and stopped. Someone opened the sliding doors next to Stone, and there stood two Gulfstream 500s.

"Which is yours?" Brio asked.

"I don't know," Stone said. As if to inform him, Faith appeared in the doorway of the jet to his left and walked down the airstairs to the tarmac.

Stone stepped out of the van and waited for Brio and Wilcox to join him.

Said excused himself. "I shall return with your quarry," he said. "In the meantime, Stone, you might see your luggage aboard."

"I need a couple of linemen," Stone said to nobody in particular.

"How about two FBI special agents?" Brio asked.

"They should do nicely. Faith, ask them to go aft and into the rear luggage compartment." He walked alongside the airplane in that direction. As he approached the exterior door to the rear luggage compartment, the door slid upward to reveal two men in business suits.

"I'll need the trunk on the left," Stone said, pointing, "and that small valise. Then you can receive our luggage from the van and go forward to the door to receive our, ah, guest."

They handed down the luggage, then took the newly arrived pieces and stowed them.

"Close the hatch as soon as everything is aboard," Stone said, then watched as they did so. Then he turned around and found himself face-to-face with Viktor Zanian, who looked pale, shrunken, and defeated. He wore shackles, hand and foot, and an armed guard stood on either side of him. Said stood next to them, smiling. "I presume those packages are for me," he said, indicating the trunk and the valise.

Stone handed him the key to the trunk. "They are. Did you bring something to replace the valise?"

Said held up a canvas carryall bag, and Stone opened the valise and emptied the contents into it. He stepped away from the trunk so that Said could have access to it.

Said knelt beside the trunk, unlocked it, and raised the lid. He smiled more broadly as he riffled through a few of the bound notes and poked around to be sure that their depth went all the way to the bottom. "So, this is what two million dollars looks like," he said.

"Exactly like that," Stone said.

Said closed and relocked the trunk and motioned for his people to take it away, then he embraced Stone.

"I hope it will not be too long before I see you again, Stone," he said.

Stone returned the embrace, then handed Said his card. "My New York address and number," he said. "I hope you will come and visit me there."

Said's two guards were carrying away the trunk. "Excuse me," the general said, "I must see that they do not carry it too far." He followed them.

Stone steered Zanian to the airstairs door and turned him over to the FBI agents. One of them held up a small suitcase. "They gave us this."

"What's in it?" Stone asked.

"A change of clothes, a toiletry bag, some prescription meds, a hair dryer, and a bottle of cognac."

"Not a problem. Walk him back to the third cabin, and shackle him to something until we've departed. We're stopping in the Azores for fuel, and you'll have to reshackle him before we land."

"Oh, and there was this," the man said, handing Stone an envelope.

Stone looked inside and found Zanian's American passport and a diplomatic passport from the Sultanate. "We'll keep this for customs and immigration," he said, handing it to Brio. "Faith, can we taxi to the runway from here?"

"Yes, we can. I've already got our clearance for Santa Maria. We have only to get permission to taxi."

"Then let's start engines and get the hell out of here," he said.

Everybody boarded and the flight attendant pulled shut the door and locked it. Stone went aft and checked on Zanian and his guards. Everything was as it should be.

He went forward, gave his jacket to the attendant, and buckled in. They were already moving.

"You look less nervous now," Brio said.

"I can't believe things went exactly as they were supposed to," Stone said. "Of course, we're not off the ground yet. Something could still go wrong."

"Ever the pessimist."

They made a turn and began their takeoff roll. Shortly, the aircraft rotated and they left the earth behind.

"Better?" Brio asked.

"Much better," Stone said, breathing deeply.

61

On the way back to the city in the Bentley, everybody was quiet. Everything had not gone as planned, but everything had finished as planned.

"Stone," Wilcox said, "you're having us for dinner tomorrow evening, correct?"

"Yes, Henry."

"May I bring a guest?"

"Of course. I'll let the cook know. It'll be black tie."

"Right," Wilcox said.

Before dinner the following evening, Stone walked the living room, dining room, and study to see that all was in order, the table set and the wine he had chosen resting on the sideboard for decanting later. Everything was perfect. He went back to the master suite, and peered into the guest dressing room. Brio was sitting at the makeup table, applying lipstick, an activity that Stone had learned, through experience, could take ten minutes. Her new badge and ID were on the table beside her. "Any word on an assignment yet?"

"Not yet. The director says he's waiting for the retirement list, so he'll know what's vacant."

"Are you a heroine at the Bureau?"

She smiled. "I am," she said, and with some satisfaction. "Nobody thought I could bring him in."

"Without Henry's quickness, Zanian would be in the wind, and with two billion dollars."

"I know. The Bureau has a banking team working to trace it all. They're optimistic that they can get most of it back to the investors."

"I wouldn't mention that to the press, until it actually happens," Stone said.

"Good advice. How many of us are we tonight?"

"The Bacchettis—Viv is here—you and I, and Henry and a guest."

"Who's the guest?"

"I didn't think to ask."

"Perhaps he has a wife stashed somewhere."

"In my experience, married men can't get through a conversation without using the phrase 'my wife.'"

Brio snorted. "I've known married men who could get through a year of conversation without using those words." She checked her lipstick again. "I'm ready."

"Then let's go down," Stone said.

They walked down to the living room and found Henry Wilcox there alone.

"Where's your guest?" Stone asked.

"Just running a little late," Wilcox replied.

Fred came into the room and handed Brio a manila envelope. "This was hand delivered a moment ago, ma'am." Brio stepped aside, opened the envelope, and examined the contents. She found a sealed envelope inside and handed it to Stone. "This is for you, marked 'personal and confidential.' It's from the director."

Stone opened the envelope, then walked toward the study. "I'll be right back," he said. He reappeared a short time later, as the doorbell rang and the Bacchettis entered.

Fred saw to the drinks, and Stone asked him to decant the wine, then he gave Viv a hug and a kiss.

"I understand you haven't been leading Dino astray," she said. "For a change."

"I don't think Dino would have liked the desert," Stone said, handing her an envelope. "You two should open this together."

Dino came over as she ripped it open and examined the contents. "Good God!" she said.

"What's the matter?" Dino asked. He took the paper from her. "Good God!" he said. "It's a check for five million dollars!"

"As promised," Stone said, patting his breast pocket. "Give me time to deposit the big one, before you cash it."

"Happy?" Brio asked.

"I've every reason to be."

"You thought we'd try to weasel out of it, didn't you?"

The doorbell prevented his answer.

"That would be my guest," Wilcox said.

Fred went to the door and came back with Lance Cabot, who knew everyone there.

"Good God!" Stone said. "It's just come to me. Henry is one of yours, isn't he?"

"Well, technically," Lance said, "he's still the ambassador to the Sultanate, but that will change tomorrow, when he starts his new job."

"Congratulations, Henry," Stone said. "What's the new job?"

Lance spoke up. "Deputy director for operations."

Henry Wilcox beamed.

END

August 27, 2021

Mount Desert Island, Maine

AUTHOR'S NOTE

I am happy to hear from readers, but you should know that if you write to me in care of my publisher, three to six months will pass before I receive your letter, and when it finally arrives it will be one among many, and I will not be able to reply.

However, if you have access to the Internet, you may visit my website at www.stuartwoods.com, where there is a button for sending me e-mail. So far, I have been able to reply to all my e-mail, and I will continue to try to do so.

If you send me an e-mail and do not receive a reply, it is probably because you are among an alarming number of people who have entered their e-mail address incorrectly in their mail software. I have many of my replies returned as undeliverable.

Remember: e-mail, reply; snail mail, no reply.

When you e-mail, please do not send attachments, as I never

open these. They can take twenty minutes to download, and they often contain viruses.

Please do not place me on your mailing lists for funny stories, prayers, political causes, charitable fund-raising, petitions, or sentimental claptrap. I get enough of that from people I already know. Generally speaking, when I get e-mail addressed to a large number of people, I immediately delete it without reading it.

Please do not send me your ideas for a book, as I have a policy of writing only what I myself invent. If you send me story ideas, I will immediately delete them without reading them. If you have a good idea for a book, write it yourself, but I will not be able to advise you on how to get it published. Buy a copy of *Writer's Market* at any bookstore; that will tell you how.

Anyone with a request concerning events or appearances may e-mail it to me or send it to: Putnam Publicity Department, Penguin Random House LLC, 1745 Broadway, New York, NY 10019.

Those ambitious folk who wish to buy film, dramatic, or television rights to my books should contact Matthew Snyder, Creative Artists Agency, 2000 Avenue of the Stars, Los Angeles, CA 90067.

Those who wish to make offers for rights of a literary nature should contact Anne Sibbald, Janklow & Nesbit, 285 Madison Avenue, 21st Floor, New York, NY 10017. (Note: This is not an invitation for you to send her your manuscript or to solicit her to be your agent.)

If you want to know if I will be signing books in your city, please visit my website, www.stuartwoods.com, where the tour schedule will be published a month or so in advance. If you wish me to do a book signing in your locality, ask your favorite bookseller to contact his Penguin representative or the Penguin publicity department with the request.

If you find typographical or editorial errors in my book and feel an irresistible urge to tell someone, please write to Gabriella Mongelli at Penguin's address above. Do not e-mail your discoveries to me, as I will already have learned about them from others.

A list of my published works appears in the front of this book and on my website. All the novels are still in print in paperback and can be found at or ordered from any bookstore. If you wish to obtain hardcover copies of earlier novels or of the two nonfiction books, a good used-book store or one of the online bookstores can help you find them. Otherwise, you will have to go to a great many garage sales.